Shadow Blight

A Shadowchasers Paranormal Romance

Seressia Glass

AUTHOR'S NOTE

This is a standalone romantic urban fantasy story set in the Shadowchasers universe. *Shadow Blight* was previously published in 2019 as *Still* in the *Christmas at Caynham Castle* anthology. It has been revised and expanded from that version.

Contents

Chapter One

Morgan plastered on a smile as the chime sounded, announcing a customer entering Lafayette's Teas and Reads. Summoning smiles grew more difficult by the day. It wasn't that she hated serving customers—quite the opposite, in fact. It was the ones who wanted readings with their spiced chais who caused her shoulders to tighten with dread.

Six weeks ago, she didn't have a problem. Six weeks ago, she didn't need the tea leaves swirling at the bottom of a cup to give a customer a reading. Six weeks ago, she'd been whole and nightmare-free and not breaking a hematite ring every three days from stress and negativity. But that was then, before her gift had fractured under the pressure of bearing witness to a gruesome murder and the taint of Shadow that had drenched it.

The door chimed again, so she smiled again. That smile froze as her mother, father, and grandmother entered the shop. For the matriarch of the Lafayette clan to come to River Street, much less downtown Savannah, wasn't all that unusual though she usually asked

Morgan to bring her something home. To have the matriarch come with Morgan's father, Senior Director of the Gilead Commission's southeast coastal region, meant something was wrong. Given the way they looked at her, that something was her.

The tea jar dropped from her grip as fear clanged through her. In what had now become an instinctive move, she wrapped shaking fingers around the faceted obsidian pendant her father had given her after the incident. Had he come as family or as a Gilead agent?

Her fight-or-flight instinct was pegged hard in the flight zone, urging her to bolt for the door. She'd have to mow her grandmother down to escape, but the three elders together could drop her on the spot with a wave of their hands. It would be foolish, futile, and fatal to oppose them, and the fact that she'd considered it even for a second told her how far gone she was.

A heavy breath slumped her shoulders as she scraped up the spilled tea leaves. "Shall we go to the office?"

Ma Belle reached into her purse. "Not before I get my espresso."

"I'll get it, Mama," her father said, putting a hand on her grandmother's arm. "Why don't y'all go on to the back? Morgan, do you want anything?"

The gentleness in her father's tone slipped through the sieve of her mental shields, threatening tears. "No, thanks."

She led her mother and grandmother to the back office, ignoring her cousin Jackie's worried expression. An expression she'd seen on nearly every Lafayette relative's face after word had spread about "The Incident." It had become easy to avoid the larger clan and only interact with her immediate family and the cousins who worked with her in the shop.

Yet Morgan couldn't ignore Jackie's reaction. Was it guilt? Was Morgan the only one in the Lafayette family who hadn't known an intervention was coming? Probably, given that her extrasense was about as reliable as a broken clock.

"This reckoning couldn't wait until I got off work?"

Tanya Lafayette settled Ma Belle into one of the four stuffed chairs circling an oval white table. Her mother then gestured for Morgan to sit and took the chair next to her. "Jackie and your staff can handle it. We're worried about you."

Morgan knew it was more than worry. Simple worry wouldn't send the head of the Lafayette clan to her tea shop in the middle of a business day. Simple worry wouldn't make her feel as if she'd been brought before a tribunal, even if it was composed of her closest relatives. Familial bonds meant nothing when Shadow was involved. A family that had walked in Light for generations couldn't tolerate Shadow in its ranks, no matter how dear the relation.

She looked at the office door, belatedly realizing how her mother had maneuvered her to the chair farthest away from the exit, blocking off her escape. *Shit.*

Her grandmother extricated a purse hook from her bottomless bag, hung it on the edge of the table, then hooked her purse straps on it. Ma Belle Lafayette would never allow her purse to rest on the floor; doing so drained your blessings. Every Lafayette woman had received an engraved hook with her first purse. Morgan never went anywhere without hers. She had no desire to test the myth.

Her grandmother reached out to cup her hand, skin the color of pecan pralines stretched tight over the gnarled bones. She rested her thumb against Morgan's wildly pounding pulse. "How are you?"

The automatic answer leaped to her tongue, forcing her to press her lips together to hold it back. She wasn't fine. She knew it, and so did they. Lying to her grandmother would be futile—that thumb over her pulse was the best lie detector in Savannah, if not the state. Probably the country.

"I'm managing," she equivocated, toying with the pendant again. It was true, as long as they didn't want to know how well or poorly she was doing it.

"Are you?" her mother asked, studying her closely. "It hasn't been that long since—"

"I know, Mama," she cut in, not wanting to hear the words. They echoed in her brain anyway. Since she'd left the hospital. Since she'd been attacked.

Since that poor girl had died.

That poor girl was Penny Halverson, a teenager abducted on her way home from school by a monster who didn't deserve to have his name remembered. The Lafayette family often helped law enforcement find the missing. Given that Morgan's extrasense enabled her to not only connect with people psychically but also find and travel to them on the astral plane, she'd been tapped to help find the teen.

Morgan had known there would be pressure to find Penny before time ran out but connecting to Penny and riding the astral winds to find her should have been simple, a routine she'd performed dozens of times over her life. Linking to Penny had been quick. So had traveling to the astral plane to find her. The young girl's extrasense had saturated the astral like a search beacon, and Morgan had been caught in it like a swimmer in an undertow. Helpless to escape, Morgan had been psychically locked to the girl during her brutal death. She'd fought free only to have her tether grabbed by the assailant—and that had been much worse.

Penny's attacker hadn't been a human monster, but a Shadow one instead—a ravenous, power-destroying beast. The Shadow creature had trapped Morgan on the astral plane, voracious and cloying, determined to steal her extrasense and extinguish her Light.

Her father had saved her by directing the authorities to the right location and pulling her free of the astral before the killer could destroy her. The encounter had left her extrasense in tatters and her soul tainted by Shadow. It had taken days to recover enough to be discharged from the hospital, days longer to stitch parts of her mental shields together to reduce the psychic static in her head to a manageable roar. The nightmares, the blight on her soul? Still there, a magic rash that wouldn't heal. Which was why she'd taken to numbing herself with painkillers and sugar cane whiskey. The combination was dangerous, but she was desperate to quiet the noise clamoring inside her skull.

"I know exactly how long it's been," she said as her father entered the office bearing a cupholder with four cups. He passed them around—espresso for Ma Belle, chai for her mother, cold green tea for himself, and a hot tea for her—before taking the empty chair beside her. She wrapped her fingers around the cup, bringing it up to inhale the steam. Chamomile, the soothing tea probably boosted with one of her father's healing spells. Unless they thought she was too far gone, in which case it might have a lulling spell on it.

"I'm trying," she told them, setting the cup aside. "I've had sessions with Bethany and with Dad. I've tried meditation and specially tuned blocking crystals. Healing isn't happening as swiftly as it should."

Her father covered her hand with his. "That's why we think you need to get away. Get away from Savannah for a couple of weeks."

Morgan stared at her family, her mouth dropping open in shock. "But it's the holidays! Take time away from Savannah, *from my shop,* in the middle of the holiday season?"

"Jackie can run the shop while you're gone," her mother said. "I can pitch in more, and I know how to follow the recipes in your tea grimoire, especially since your father and I helped write some of them."

"Being away means missing Christmas. You want me to miss a Lafayette Christmas?" she asked, aware of her voice climbing. "Not even the mayor misses a Lafayette Christmas!"

Ma Belle gave her a look, one that had made her sit straight and mind her manners since she was a toddler. "You act as if this is a suggestion."

Morgan winced at the iron threading her grandmother's words. Going against the matriarch's orders wasn't an option, but she still turned to her parents, desperate for a reprieve. Tanya Lafayette had left her Romani family to marry Morgan's father, but she'd added her own gifts to the powerful Lafayette bloodline, making her an accepted and respected part of the family. Her parents together were a formidable team, like pattern-welded steel wrapped in southern cotton, *#relationshipgoals*. Morgan dreamed of having something close to what her parents had, but it was a dream deferred by the nightmare her life had become.

"We agree with your grandmother," Tanya Lafayette said, her eyes shining with unshed tears. "It's the best option we have right now."

Cold fog formed in her chest, causing her shoulders to slump. Her nearest and dearest wanted to send her away as if she were an embarrassment that needed to be hidden. "There's nothing I can say to change your minds?"

Ma Belle brushed her thumb across Morgan's pulse before her mother could answer. "Do you remember what happened to Cousin Laney?"

The quiet question dropped like a bomb in the tiny room. For Ma Belle to mention her late niece... Morgan's hope plummeted. "I remember."

Every Lafayette relative knew the story of Cousin Laney, mainly because the elders used it as a cautionary tale for the younger generations. For others, like Morgan, it was a recent memory. Though she'd been little more than a first grader then, with her grandmother as the matriarch and her father set to become the patriarch, she'd lived all her life in Lafayette House, the Lafayette mansion and family seat. Ma Belle's sister and her family had also lived there, which meant Morgan had witnessed firsthand Cousin Laney's descent into Shadow-madness. The elders of the family had attempted all they could to help Laney, to heal her, then restrained her.

When Laney had gotten loose and terrorized the youngest children in the mansion, including Morgan's younger brother, Gregory, the family realized they could no longer contain Laney. Ma Belle had made the decision to contact the Gilead Commission, the governing body for all things Light, hoping they would send someone to help. Instead of sending a Light healer, a Shadowchaser had arrived in Savannah. The family still didn't know what had happened to Cousin Laney. Her parents and siblings had left the mansion, and Emma, Ma Belle's sister, had gone into seclusion.

"It's hard to forget something like that. Gregory hasn't come home in years, except for Christmas day to see you, Mom, and Dad. And Auntie Emma is still a recluse to this day."

Her elders exchanged loaded glances. A cold knot formed at the base of her spine. "What is it?"

"My sister is no longer in seclusion," Ma Belle said. "She heard about what happened with you and reported it to Gilead. They contacted your father for more information."

"What?" Morgan's breath caught as she shrank back in her chair, her heart hammering so hard she was sure they could all hear it. Of course, her grandaunt knew what had happened to her. It was hard to keep secrets in a family full of psychics and Light Adepts.

It wasn't a surprise that the Gilead Commission knew about her encounter. They had agents everywhere. The fact that her grandaunt had reported her reeked of retribution. That Gilead, in turn, had contacted her father for an explanation as if he, in his capacity as a Gilead director, had hidden her situation didn't bode well, especially for her. Then there was her grandmother's peculiar phrasing: what happened *with* her, not *to* her, as if she bore responsibility for Penny's death and her own near-fatal encounter with the Shadow-cursed killer.

Her grandmother sighed. "My sister has lived on resentment and revenge since we lost her daughter. Her action isn't a surprise."

Ma Belle grabbed Morgan's wrist in an iron grip. "Besides, Gilead already knew what had happened with you because Darien told them right after the attack."

But they had contacted her father again. Fear, true and undeniable, slid like a death-cold hand down her back. Had they already decided her fate? Was a Shadowchaser already on the way?

She half-rose from her chair, body shaking. "You keep saying what happened with me instead of to me, as if I were a willing participant and not violated against my will!"

"Morgan—"

She ignored her mother, too scared, too angry to hold the words back. "The first time you called them, did they apologize for not sending agents to handle that monster? If Gilead is so all-knowing, why didn't they send a Shadowchaser to destroy that Shadow-drenched thing instead of sending one after me like they did Cousin Laney? If they'd done their jobs from the jump, I wouldn't have been trapped and nearly killed by that son of a bitch, and you wouldn't be trying to get rid of me like rancid garbage to make Auntie Emma happy!"

"Enough!"

Power rolled through the room as Ma Belle slammed her hand down on the table. Morgan ducked her head, collapsing into her chair, the rage she'd been nurturing for weeks evaporating beneath the force of her grandmother's magic. "I'm sorry, but—"

The Lafayette matriarch turned to her, eyes glowing, her voice a chorus of their ancestors. "If you don't know, don't act like you know. And do not sit there throwing a tantrum like a frightened child instead of standing in grace and Light as a Lafayette should."

Tears fractured Morgan's vision as remorse punched her hard. She would have fallen to her knees if there had been room, so she rested her forehead against the tabletop instead. "Forgive me, ancestors. Forgive me, matriarch. Forgive me, Mother and Father. Fear made me forget my blood."

Her blood bore the Light magic of the generations who had come before her. They all, men and women, had faithfully walked in Light. None had turned to Shadow voluntarily, not even Laney. She wouldn't either, but she could feel the Shadow trying to dim her Light, overcoming it bit by tiny bit.

She balled her hands into fists, choking back her wildly swinging emotions. Being a Lafayette meant being a powerful beacon of Light, helping others stand against Shadow. The family calling had been ingrained in her in childhood, almost before she'd learned the alphabet. If she couldn't be of service, if she didn't have her gifts, what else was left? Nothing. She'd be left with nothing, all because she hadn't known that she faced an adversary better left to Gilead and their deadly enforcers.

She waited, hoping the ancestors would forgive her. Finally, her grandmother placed a hand on the top of Morgan's head. "Dealing with the fallout from the attack hasn't been easy for you, child. Let your elders help you."

Her mother hugged her shoulders to pull her upright. "You need time to heal, and we need to defuse the situation with your aunt, which means you need time away from Savannah. Someplace with a powerful healer, powerful Light magic, and no one named Lafayette. Solace."

Tears pricked her eyes. Solace. She wanted it, craved it. A Light-filled place with a powerful healer to cure her. And it would be good to take a break from the cacophony of holidays in Savannah. Despite her love of her hometown, it was crawling with Lafayettes, and she didn't want to face the added stress caused by Auntie Emma stirring the pot.

She looked at her father, really looked. He had never told her what he'd experienced saving her from the astral plane, and she'd been afraid to ask. The silver patch of crinkled hair at his right temple told the story. He'd paid a heavy price, one that she could never reimburse him for.

They all had. Through her own misery, she could clearly see their worry, their concern for her and the family. It wasn't just her well-being on the line. "I don't want you at odds with the Gilead Commission, Dad, just as I don't want Ma Belle at odds with her sister. If leaving will help, I'll do it. But will Gilead allow me to leave?"

"Your injury is different from Lanney's Shadow madness," her father said, "which I very clearly explained to upper management in the southeast branch. They agreed that it's fine for you to leave."

Morgan reached for her tea, honey-sweetened just the way she liked it. Having Gilead and her grandmother in agreement had to mean that they were all hopeful she could be cured, right? "I suppose y'all have a place in mind where you want me to go?"

Ma Belle reached into her purse and extracted a brochure. "Here."

A tinge of energy singed Morgan's fingertips as she accepted the brochure from her grandmother. The elegant script at the top proclaimed: *Experience the Magic of Caynham Castle*. A grayish-tan stone castle rose against a gray-blue sky, not quite like the grandiose structures of fairytales. No, this one was not for show unless it was a show of strength, hunkering down and weathering anything thrown at it.

She flipped open the sales brochure, noting elegantly appointed suites, a gorgeous solarium, and lush greenery leading to a sinuous river. She also noted the location and looked up at her grandmother, incredulous. "You want me to vacation in a castle. In a place called Caynham-on-Led...Ledwyche. I don't even know how to pronounce that or where it is."

"It's in Shropshire, England," her father helpfully clarified.

"A castle in England for Christmas." *Was this really happening?*

"It's supposed to be a very soothing, peaceful area," her mother told her. "Of course, if you choose to be more festive, there's going to be some sort of gala there during Christmas week."

Morgan focused on two words: soothing and peaceful. She needed that even if she couldn't admit it aloud. Besides, her elders knew the truth already. "It seems like a nice place. Walking along the river, there will be a completely different experience from strolling River Street here, but there's no way they still have an open room this close to the holiday."

"Actually," her grandmother said in a tone that clanged in Morgan's ratty extrasense. "It just so happens that they had one suite left. I booked it for you."

Shock raced through her again as she slumped back in her chair. So many questions swirled through her. How had her grandmother discovered this castle? How recently had she booked the room? How long had they been planning to get rid of her?

She dropped her gaze to the table's surface, not wanting to show the pain all three of them knew sawed through her. "When am I leaving?" she asked through a tight throat. "I'm assuming you've bought my airfare too?"

"Yes." Her father then dropped the bombshell. "You fly out the day after tomorrow."

Two days. In two days, she had to leave her life behind. "How long are you sending me away for?"

"At least until the end of the year."

She flinched despite every effort not to. Her grandmother's words lacerated the fragile façade she'd shown the world since she'd come home from the hospital. The matriarch's meaning was clear: if she couldn't get herself together, if she wasn't able to heal, she wouldn't be able to come back to the family. The Lafayettes didn't need another family member falling into Shadow.

"Morgan." Her father took her hand again. "We know you've tried to heal and recover. Every member of the family who could help has tried. Meghan didn't give us details, but we know you had therapy sessions with her as well."

"How is being sent away from my business and my family during Christmas supposed to help?" she asked, choked. "You sure you're not getting rid of me because I'm irreparably broken and susceptible to falling into Shadow?"

"No, baby, no." Her mother pulled her against her chest. "We want you to get better, and we think this will help."

"How?"

"There's a Light Adept who lives near the castle in Caynham-on-Ledwyche. Her name is Margaret Davies, but she goes by Meg. She has an antiques shop there called Curiouser & Curiouser."

She straightened with a choked snort. "A Light Adept with an *Alice in Wonderland* fixation."

"Meg Davies is also a healer," her grandmother said, frowning at her sarcasm. "She happens to specialize in healing psychic wounds, particularly those caused by Shadow. I've known her for years, and I know the power she wields. She's the best in England, if not all of Europe. She's expecting you."

Morgan froze. Something unfurled in her chest, too tiny and frail to be called hope. "Do you really think there's a chance she can heal me?"

Ma Belle's expression softened. "We wouldn't send you there if we didn't."

"Think of it this way, my beautiful daughter." Morgan's mother framed her cheeks with her hands. "My princess gets to spend the holidays in a castle. The best present is for you to be all healed by the new year."

"Okay." That tiny thing in her chest fluttered again, gaining strength. "Okay. Let's do this."

Chapter Two

I f she'd needed more proof that this trip was the proverbial Hail Mary, the eight-hour overnight flight from Atlanta to Birmingham, England, was more than enough. Too afraid to sleep and open herself to a nightmare, or worse, a psychic attack she couldn't defend against, Morgan had kept the obsidian pendant in a death-grip while watching Korean dramas. Even so, she remained hyperaware of everything around her. Too many people, too many voices, too much noise inside her head. Fomenting chaos, feeding the taint of Shadow chewing at the frayed edges of her extrasense. The clamoring beat against her skull, transforming her into a pressure cooker, with no idea how far away she was from bursting.

The fragile hope she'd had at the end of the intervention had died the same night, killed by the same violent nightmare of her astral attack. Why the matriarch had allowed her to come unescorted eluded her. Maybe they believed she wasn't as far gone as she felt.

She hadn't relinquished the fear of losing control until she'd gathered her bags and rendezvoused with the driver she'd hired to take her to Caynham-on-Ledwyche. Shutting out the outside world and settling into the quiet interior of the car had been a relief. So, too, had been leaving Birmingham and heading northwest to Shropshire. Less people meant less noise, and she was able to put in her earbuds and focus on the pendant and the Light meditation techniques her mother had taught her to achieve a veneer of inner peace. No need to call a Shadowchaser on her. Yet.

Her destination rose above the trees and rooftops of the town like a gray-gold beast hulking against the late afternoon misty sky. Caynham Castle. She'd read up on her temporary home during the flight. It had been built sometime in the thirteenth century, and an actual earl and his family still owned it, although they lived in a manor house nearby. The castle had been converted to a hotel around 1920 and hosted a ton of events, including weddings. She hoped the amenities in her suite were more recent than in the previous century.

The driver turned off the road and onto a gravel lot in front of a massive wall. "Here we are, miss."

Morgan rubbed at her bleary, sleep-deprived eyes. Thanking the driver, she settled her bill as a young man wearing a windbreaker bearing the hotel's name and logo opened her door. "Welcome to the Caynham Castle Hotel," he said, holding an umbrella for her. "I'll get your luggage. If you'll come this way, I have a cart to take you to registration."

A cart? She exited the car and spied a covered golf cart idling close by, then immediately comprehended why it was necessary. Her rideshare had stopped in a gravel parking lot. A massive wall seemed to stretch forever to the right but was broken by a large archway on the left. From this angle, she couldn't see anything of the castle, much less the hotel part of it. Then, the cart trundled through the arch, and Caynham Castle transformed from a forbidding fortress into a holiday wonderland. Lights festooned the trees, giving everything a warm glow. A giant tent dominated the greenspace, and workers scurried in and out, erecting a variety of structures.

"Wow, there's a lot of activity going on."

"Yes, miss. Aside from our regular holiday decorations, which went up a few weeks ago, everyone's hard at work preparing for the Flame and Frost ball this coming weekend. Will you be attending?"

"I have tickets for it." She wasn't sure why her parents and grand-mother thought she'd want to go to the ball, but she'd been in no mood to argue. Of course, she had no idea what frame of mind she'd be in by the night of the ball or even if she'd have much of a mind left. On top of that, she hadn't packed a dress, and with something called a ball being held Christmas weekend at a castle, she didn't think she could find anything fancy enough to wear, especially on short notice.

"If you're looking for something a bit more traditional, we'll have a Christmas Eve service at the church in town, and then everyone will come back here for the bell-ringing event at midnight."

"That sounds lovely. Thank you for letting me know."

"Of course. If you need anything else, just ask for Johnny."

The cart slowed, and she realized that a collection of multi-storied stone buildings integrated into the inside of the wall. The young man stopped in front of one, its entryway adorned with lighted potted trees and garland. She pulled her own umbrella from her leather backpack, grabbed one of her cases, and followed the porter inside to registration.

The lighted trees outside had merely been a hint of what the interior entailed. More potted firs adorned with lights and red bows sat in every open nook and cranny. Red-ribboned garlands draped the carved wooden counter, and soft holiday instrumental music filled the air. The bright and festive ambience triggered a sharp stab of homesickness. Lafayette House, the Victorian that had been the family seat for multiple generations, was decorated with the same exuberance down to the wreaths attached to the haint blue shutters. She'd miss the annual Christmas Eve family gathering with all the Lafayette cousins, getting up early the next day with her grandmother and others to cook breakfast and then prep for the massive holiday dinner. Yes, they could have catered, given how many mouths they fed, but there was a reason why an invite from the Lafayette matriarch was a hot commodity in the community.

Another pang of sadness hit her. It was her own fault she'd been sent away. As gorgeous as Caynham Castle was, a beautiful exile was still an exile.

"Are you all right?"

Morgan dredged up a smile for the bespectacled, brown-haired woman peering with concern at her from behind the counter. "Just tired from traveling," she responded. "I'm hoping my room is ready."

"Let's have a look. May I have your name and identification, please?"

Morgan handed over her passport and credit card. "Morgan Lafayette."

The woman, whose nametag declared her to be Constance, gave her a bright smile. "Are you named for our famous enchantress?"

"Actually, I'm named for my great-grandfather," she answered, "but the tie-in to Morgan le Fay is why my mother went along with it."

"If magic's what you want, I suggest strolling about in our gorgeous scenery," Constance told her, producing a brochure that opened into a map of the grounds. "As you can see, there's plenty to take in here at the castle. The Folly is stunning, as are the chapel and the conservatory.

There are plenty of hiking paths and cycling available. No proof of magical ability required."

"That's a relief." She wasn't certain she could perform magic on demand at the moment anyway. "Is the restaurant open?"

Constance pointed at the map. "Lady Neville's Tearoom is here, and it will serve afternoon tea in half an hour. The restaurant in the Great Hall opens in two hours. Of course, we have pubs and another teashop or two in town."

Morgan measured her energy reserves against waiting for the main restaurant to open or making the walk into town. Her throbbing head gave her the answer. "I'll have afternoon tea. That will give me time to unpack."

"Excellent." Constance handed over her room key. "Your room is here, on the first floor. You can reach the lift by following this corridor."

Morgan blinked in confusion, then nodded. Right. She was in Britain. The lobby level was the ground floor, and the next one up was the first. It had been a couple of years since her last European trip, and her brain was too muddled to make the swift adjustment. "Thank you."

"You're quite welcome. Enjoy your stay."

Deciding to take the well-wishes to heart, Morgan made her way to the elevator. She could choose to regard this trip as an exile or self-care, a chance to relax, rejuvenate, and heal. Viewing this excursion in a positive light would put her in the proper mindset to fight the taint of Shadow on her psyche, and she needed all the help she could get.

She found her room easily enough. It was a blend of contemporary conveniences and antique artistry. The carved headboard and crisp white linens on the bed were softened by the gorgeous, handmade quilt. An equally impressive tapestry adorned the wall behind the bed.

A painting of the castle in its heyday took pride of place on the outer wall. Small, leaded windows looked out onto what the brochure called the outer ward with its massive tent, and just beyond that, she could make out a second wall with a large, decorated tree and the castle proper just beyond.

It was a relief to find the bathroom outfitted with modern fixtures. After handling her business, she began to unpack, pausing when she saw a stuffed garment bag carefully folded into her largest case. She didn't remember packing it, focused as she was on necessities like her healing crystals and haircare products. Curious, she placed the garment bag flat on the bed then unzipped it.

Crimson-red fabric with glittering embellishments spilled out to reveal a ballgown, one she certainly did not own. A piece of paper caught her attention, the printed trail of red roses signifying her mother's stationery. The note simply said, *Something bright to look forward to. Love you much, Mom.*

Morgan's vision blurred as she carefully stowed the gown away. If things went well, if Meg Davies was able to heal her, then going to the holiday ball wearing that fantastic ball gown would be her reward. Something to look forward to, indeed. "Thank you, Mom."

She still needed to protect herself in her temporary home. The last thing she unpacked from her carry-on was an intricately carved wooden box. She took it over to the antique writing desk and sat down. After taking several cleansing breaths, she centered herself, set her intention, then opened the case to reveal an assortment of crystals and a glass atomizer of sage oil spray. The stones were from a cousin who personally traveled to look for stones for her metaphysical gift shop, who had curated a set of stones to guard her sleep. Her mother had charged four palm-sized clear quartz, and the spray was from another cousin with an aromatherapy practice that had become famous when a top actress filming in Savannah bought some for herself and the entire crew.

Morgan walked the room, chanting as she went. "May the Light bless this place. May the Light fill this space. May the Light keep Shadow at bay. May the Light keep me safe."

She placed a clear quartz crystal in each corner of the room, repeating the chant as she spritzed all four corners and the window. She then placed the curated collection on the nightstand in a specific array, except for a tumbled lepidolite and an obsidian shard which she placed beneath her pillow. Hopefully, those stones, combined with the energy of her black tourmaline pendant, would be enough to keep the nightmares at bay.

Holding her breath, she touched a fingertip to the point of clear quartz in the center of the arrangement on the nightstand, then fed a tendril of extrasense into it. She squeaked in excited surprise as the crystal activated, its energy rushing out to connect with the corners on a beam of blue-white light. Each ray flowed up the walls like a reversed waterfall, meeting in the center of the ceiling to form a protective cage of Light energy.

Grateful, she thanked the Light for the blessing before pulling out her phone to video call her parents. They'd worry if she didn't inform them of her safe arrival. "Hi, Dad. Is now a good time?"

"Anytime is a good time to talk to my baby girl," he said with a laugh. "We've been waiting for your call. Hold on, and I'll conference your mother in."

She settled into the plush guest chair beneath the painting as she waited for her mother to join them. Soon enough, her mother's smiling visage joined her father's on the screen. "Morgan! I'm so glad you made it safely. How was your flight?"

"Uneventful."

Concern wrapped her mother's features. "You sound tired, and you look exhausted. Did you get any sleep on the plane?"

Morgan didn't have the energy to evade the question. "No. I didn't think it would be smart to sleep on the flight, considering the state of my shields and my extrasense. I've cleansed the room and set my crystals, and I'm going to crash as soon as I get something to eat. There's something called afternoon tea that I'm hoping has something more than Earl Grey and tiny cakes."

"If not, I'm sure you can have something delivered," her father said. "How do you like it so far? Does it feel like you're staying in an actual castle?"

"I haven't seen much of it yet, but it's definitely a castle." She held up the phone so that they could see her room, followed by the view outside the window. "They're going all out for the holiday, and the ball coming up."

Her mother gasped. "You're going to attend?"

Morgan stared at the garment bag draped over the valet stand. "I kind of have to, don't I, since you bought me that dress? I don't know how you managed to find something so beautiful in my size on short notice."

"We all have our talents, dear," her mother answered with a smug smile. "I'm glad you've changed your mind about attending the ball. I think it will be a wonderful distraction for you."

"I could definitely use a distraction," she said, rubbing at her forehead. "Besides, maybe my session with the Light healer tomorrow will go so well that I'll have a reason to kick up my heels and dance."

"That's my girl," her father said, his tone approving. "No matter what, you deserve the chance to have some fun."

"It's true," her mother added. "You've worked so hard since you took over the store from me, making it your own. When was the last time you had a real vacation?"

"I..." She frowned, trying to think. Running a small business left little free time for anything else. Add in her familial obligations and occasional aid to the police, any time she had left was used for sleep. Unless she counted the time spent recovering in the hospital, she hadn't had any time off until now.

"All right," she caved. "I promise to troop around to all the tourist sites and take lots of photos in between my sessions with Mrs. Davies. That will start tomorrow, though. Sunset happens a lot earlier here during winter than it does back home. That should help me sleep like a log tonight after I get back from the teahouse."

Not wanting to think about the night ahead, Morgan abruptly changed the subject. "Speaking of teashops, how's ours doing?"

"We've had a great morning rush and a couple of readings," her mother answered, her expression brightening. "We've got more scheduled for the rest of the week. It feels good to be in the store helping customers again."

Morgan swallowed a pang of jealousy. No, she hadn't hoped the shop would fall apart without her, but it would have been nice if her absence was felt. "You'll need to mix up more of the caramel rooibos blend. We were running low over the weekend, and I—"

"I know. You told me yesterday morning when we reviewed the inventory software."

"That was yesterday?" She rubbed at her forehead. It felt like days ago. Everything was a jumble in her head.

"Morgan." Her father's voice snagged her attention. "The shop is in good hands. You know this. The most important thing for you right now is food then rest so that you can be in good shape for your appointment with Mrs. Davies. Do you have the details?"

"Yes. According to the email, I'm supposed to meet her tomorrow at eleven at her antiques shop, Curiouser & Curiouser."

"Good." Her father leaned closer to the phone. "Sweetheart, it's important for you to be in the right frame of mind for your sessions with Mrs. Davies. We have faith in you."

"We're sending all the positive vibes we have your way," her mother added, "along with our prayers. We believe in you."

Tears blurred her vision. "I won't fail you," she promised. "I won't fail myself."

"We know you won't."

They said their goodbyes, then disconnected. Morgan slumped down in the chair, one arm over her eyes. The pressure to heal, to recover her abilities, sat like an anchor on her chest, oppressive and overwhelming. So much rested on her encounter with Meg Davies, a woman she didn't know but whom she had to trust with the very essence of herself.

She found a tissue to blot at her eyes, then rose with a sigh, rubbing at her forehead and the headache that seemed omnipresent these days. One day at a time, one step at a time. The next step: food.

She made her way downstairs to Lady Neville's tearoom, a space inside the castle's outer wall made quaint with a motley assortment of chairs and tables and mismatched tableware. As enticing as the three-course tea was, she found her appetite fading as quickly as her energy. At least she had enough on her stomach to take something for her headache. Squashing the need to apologize, she quickly settled her bill before returning to her room.

Running on fumes, she readied herself for bed, putting her hair into twists and securing them in a satin wrap before taking a shower.

Dried, dressed, and moisturized, she placed her phone on its charger then pulled back the covers before sliding into bed. While she couldn't see the magical grid protecting the room, she could feel it like a kitten curled on her chest. Hopefully, the stones would do their job and give her the peaceful rest she desperately needed. Meeting with Meg Davies after breakfast would take care of the rest. It had to. She was staying in a castle during the season of miracles, but she knew she wasn't a princess. No matter how much she believed in magic and miracles, she doubted a white knight would charge in to slay the Shadow coiling in her body.

***

Morgan blinked awake. Darkness still filled the window, punctuated by the softly glowing holiday lights gleaming from the tree in the middle bailey.

She frowned. She couldn't see the tree while lying down. Why was she seeing it now?

Attempting to sit up, she pushed against the mattress for leverage. The mattress wasn't there. She looked down to see herself curled beneath the coverlet, an ethereal cord, glowing a soft white, rising up from her sacral chakra to connect to her astral body.

Her astral body.

Exhilaration swept through her, banishing fatigue. It had been months since she'd been able to reach the astral, and all it had taken was being so bone-weary she hadn't been able to think about it.

Joy lifted her up to the ceiling, then twisted into trepidation. Her last journey to the astral had trapped her and left a literal mark on her psyche. If she got trapped again, with her father an ocean away...

No. She had to stay positive. She was miles and miles, literally and figuratively, from that dark moment. Traveling here should be safe, but she'd quickly retreat to the physical plane at the first sign of trouble. She looked down at her body again, at the gleaming tether. Assured that the connection was secure, she decided to explore.

Up and out of the castle's confines, she could see the energies that imbued the grounds. There was magic here, ancient and wild and mostly sleeping. She flew up and out, leaving the physical plane behind, her extrasense noting the shimmering curtain of energy separating the planes. She hadn't spontaneously traveled since puberty and hadn't been able to voluntarily travel at all in the weeks following "The Incident." To be able to do so now, here…there were no words. Words weren't necessary in the astral, and she gave herself over to the current, drawing on the Light energy that pulsed like an aurora.

A blip in the current snagged her attention. She focused on a pinprick of light then zoomed in. The light resolved into a literal knight in shining armor.

A Light guardian? She knew protective entities existed. They hadn't done much for her when the Shadow creature had killed Penny and attacked her. It was her father who had saved her, not a Light guardian, and she felt some type of way about that.

The knight faced her, his sword extended out to the side. "I cannot allow you to pass, fair maiden," he said, the unspoken words a current between them. "That way be dragons."

"Then I suppose it's a good thing that I'm neither fair nor a maiden," she quipped, then started forward again.

Again, he blocked her, his sword glowing brighter. "It isn't safe to continue that way."

Morgan drew up. "Because of the dragon." She'd never encountered such a creature during her astral travels, but just because she hadn't met one didn't mean they didn't exist. If he claimed there was a dragon, she'd take his word for it. "So you're a Light protector for the astral plane?"

The knight nodded. "It is my duty and my calling."

"So where were you when I needed you?"

The words burst from her, jangling the space between them. The discord reverberated back to her, causing her to wobble.

The knight sheathed his sword before removing his helmet, revealing decidedly human facial features. He stretched out a hand. "You're wounded."

Morgan's shrank back as the Shadow-mark between her shoulder blades throbbed with her pain and anguish. "Of course I'm wounded! I tried to do the right thing and got injured for my trouble."

The knight's energy reached out to her, but she danced back. "I was trapped on the astral plane. I nearly died. My father had to come save me. Where were you? Why didn't you protect me?"

Anguish pulsed again, not hers this time. "I didn't know. If I did, I would have helped. Please believe me."

Morgan wrenched her anger and anguish back down. His words didn't sound like that of a Light guardian. He sounded more...human. She drew back, clasping her hands to her chest. "You're human."

His eyes, a blazing deep blue, reflected the shock she felt. He moved closer. "You're a true traveler as well, not an accidental one? Who are you? Where are you?"

A trumpeting roar rolled through the astral. A chill jangled along Morgan's cord. Something approached. Something dark and dangerous.

The knight freed his sword. "You should go, fair maiden," he said. "Light willing, I'll find you again."

"But I can—"

"Go!"

He thrust out a hand. An invisible wave of power hit her, sending her tumbling head over heels, speeding along the astral back to the physical realm. She landed in her body with a thud that had her jerking upright, gasping for air.

What the hell had just happened? She rarely met other travelers, certainly not one who channeled so much Light magic that she'd mistake them for a Guardian. What did that dark, trumpeting sound herald? He'd mentioned a dragon. Did he mean that literally?

Did it matter? She couldn't leave him on the astral to face whatever that was on his own. Even though it terrified her, she wasn't one to run. Lying back, she closed her eyes, reaching for the astral. Nothing. She tried again, imagining light infusing her body, the silver cord unfurling, the physical world falling away.

Nothing.

"Dammit!" She pounded the mattress in frustration. Failure pressed down on her. The knight needed her help to face whatever that dark disturbance was. Even if he didn't, it went against everything she and her family stood for to abandon someone. All she could do was send up prayers that the knight would be safe and victorious. In the morning, she'd open up to Meg Davies, get healed, then return to the astral to search for her mystery knight.

Chapter Three

· ·

Fortified by a hearty breakfast in the Great Hall and armed with waterproof hiking boots and directions on her phone, Morgan was ready to start her walk to Caynham-on-Ledwyche, the village just outside the castle grounds. The castle went all out for the holiday season, more than she'd imagined. Not only was there a huge Christmas tree in the ballroom, but there were also several smaller ones in the restaurant and flanking the entryway. All of them paled in comparison to the great tree in the castle's second yard—what someone told her was called the inner bailey. Most of the frost had melted away, but the air still had a bright crispness to it that kept her from being too warm in her leather jacket.

Giddiness added pep to her step as she crossed the wide expanse of the outer bailey housing a massive tent. She'd traveled the astral last night. It would have been easy to dismiss it as a lucid dream born of wishful thinking, but she knew different. The buzz she felt whenever she projected had been there, although muted. Everything about the experience had been vivid, all of her senses engaged as they were when she was awake. Then there was her encounter with the knight...

Her steps slowed as she approached the ancient two-lane stone bridge that connected the castle to the town. She looked at the pale winter sunlight glinting off the dappled surface of the river, but her thoughts had turned inward. The knight was human, she was sure of it. A human with an incredibly powerful well of Light magic. Who was he? Where was he? Most importantly, was he safe?

Keeping to the pedestrian path, Morgan crossed over the bridge and followed Caynham Castle Road into the outskirts of town. Perhaps Mrs. Davies would know about the mystery magic man. Davies had to be plugged into the magical community in this country for the Lafayette matriarch to contact her. She had to know a male magic user with that level of power. She'd describe her astral experience from the night before, then ask about the knight. If she was lucky, the healer would give her information about her mystery man—and take Morgan's spontaneous travel as a sign that she was on the mend.

With her plan of action set, Morgan turned her attention back to her surroundings. Even with her extrasense muted, she could feel the buzz of the land's energy. It hummed with nearly the same frequency she'd experienced during her astral travel the night before, the music of old memory and older magic. Maybe the knight was able to draw on the magic of land the way she could sometimes draw on the power of the Savannah River. It would be awesome to compare magical notes if she could find him.

Caynham-on-Ledwyche was a beautiful blend of almost-modern and medieval, no doubt thanks to some strong preservation ordinances. Brick and stone edifices stood next to multi-storied white buildings with dark timber trim. She could well imagine what it must have been like a couple of centuries ago, with most of these buildings standing then as they did now.

Morgan pulled up a map on her phone to orient herself. Curiouser and Curiouser sat on a street named Knight Road, which forked off the main throughway. She tried not to read too much into that, but she still took it as a positive sign, one in a series of soon-to-come fortunate events. Aside from the antiques and oddities shop, there were other shops and a pub along the same road, including a yarn shop she knew she'd have to return to. Cousin Emmett had a respectable online shop selling hand-knitted wares imbued with healing spells. He was sure to appreciate some locally-produced yarn.

Holiday lights and garland framed one window showcasing a tray of baubles. She skidded to a stop for a closer look, not at the sparkling jewelry but the scarf the tray rested on. It shimmered as if silk, painted in a series of blue, green, and purple squiggles that almost formed words if she could only peruse it from the right perspective. It called to her, but she wasn't sure if it was a "buy me" compulsion or a "you need me" declaration. Only one way to find out.

She pushed open the door and stepped inside, pulling her gloves off to stuff into her jacket pocket. A man stood behind the glass counter, helping a pair of customers finalize their purchases. He called out a greeting, but she paid little heed, her focus scattered by the energies in the shop fizzing along her senses like just-opened champagne. A motley mix of items crammed every available nook and cranny, but she lingered by the display in the window, staring at the scarf. It chittered at her in much the way a happy parakeet would, and she longed to cup it in her hands, press her cheek against the cool fabric, and become acquainted with it. No matter the price, she wasn't leaving the shop without it.

She glanced up briefly as the other customers left. "Excuse me, sir?"

"Something in the window catch your eye?" he asked as he approached.

"Ah, yes," she began, turning around. "I'd like to see the..."

Shock barreled through her as she faced the man. It was him! The knight from her astral dream. Instead of shining armor, he wore a dark gray sweater and navy trousers. His eyes...his eyes were unmistakable, deeply blue beneath a sweep of dark blond hair.

What were the odds? How was he in front of her, in the flesh, working in Meg Davies' shop? Dumbfounded and in need of distance to think, she wobbled back a step. He immediately reached out to steady her, capturing her hand in a firm grip.

Magic flared like a sparkler, warm and bright with purple-white light and a low bass thrum that reverberated inside her. After it faded, silence fell, thicker than that in the center of a wild forest, rolling out from their clasped hands to create a quiet cocoon around them.

His grip on her hand tightened, recognition crashing through his gaze. "Are you—is it really you? My fair maiden from the astral?"

His hushed recognition only served to unnerve her more. Needing to regroup, she snatched her hand free. Big mistake.

The quiet cloak of his magic collapsed like an imploding building, allowing the noise she'd thought vanquished by her night's rest to crash back in. Groaning, her equilibrium rocked, she clutched her head as the rumble increased to a roar. Worse, so much worse. Her shields stretched, then popped, too tattered to contain the cacophony of noise, magic, Light, and Shadow bombarding her. The mark on her back burned.

Panic joined pain, and she bit back a cry but could do nothing as the world went gray around the edges.

***

Arthur muttered a curse as he caught the woman when she sagged, firmly locking down his shields so as not to unbalance her again. His heart pounded as he guided her behind the counter and into the back room to settle in a plush chair, then hurried to the front door to lock up. Holiday sales would have to wait.

Returning to the back room, he tended to the woman as best he could, pressing a glass of water into her hand, wishing he had some tea at the ready. She roused, lifting the glass with trembling hands to take one sip then another before handing the glass back to him. Careful not to brush his fingers against hers, he took it and then placed it on the table. Hoping he hadn't scared her, he kneeled in front of her as she rubbed at her temples and gripped a black stone pendant in turn.

He swallowed another curse, recognizing the pendant as a protection amulet. How could he have made such a childish mistake, allowing his magic to wash over her? His only excuse was that her astral projection had attracted him like a compass to true north, so it was natural that their magics would attract each other here on the physical plane. He hadn't realized that he'd unshielded, so stunned was he to see her in person. The astral traveler in the flesh, angelic but not a shimmering angel as he'd seen her the night before. A beautiful American, no doubt here on holiday, with a riot of brown and copper coily hair framing dark chocolate eyes.

"Are you all right? Do you need me to phone anyone for you?" He held his hands out, wanting to touch her again but not daring to unless she toppled over. He'd ring his mother if the stranger needed further help. That call and its reason wouldn't go over well with his healer mother, but he'd suffer the consequences to make sure the tourist was all right.

"Thank you, but there's no need to call anyone," she answered. "I'm fine. More embarrassed than anything."

Yes, definitely American, with an accent as sweet and flowing as the local honey produced by the castle. "As am I. It wasn't my intention to shock you."

A smile bowed her lips in an absolutely delightful way. "We were both shocked. I certainly didn't expect to walk into a gift shop to find my knight in astral shining armor behind the counter."

He took extreme pleasure in the way she said, "My knight." Way more pleasure than he should have. "I didn't expect my glimmering angel to walk into my shop today," he replied, then admitted, "but I'm glad you did. I haven't encountered many travelers on the astral, I'm sorry to say."

"Neither have I." She studied him. "I didn't think you were real at first. Well, not human real anyway. A knight in shining armor? I thought you might have been a Light guardian, a manifestation sent to protect me, which is why I lashed out at you. I apologize for that."

"No need. I thought you were a lucid dreamer." Curiosity burned his tongue. "I have so many questions. It's been so long since I've met another human out on the astral. Are you truly an at-will traveler, or do you journey spontaneously? Do you know any other travelers? Do you have any other Light magic?"

"Whoa." She held up her hands, and he immediately scooted backward to give her space. "Shouldn't we at least exchange names first?"

"Forgive me for being rude." He stood to put proper distance between them. "May I ask your name?"

"It's Morgan." She hesitated a moment before adding, "Lafayette."

He wasn't going to make the joke she no doubt expected. Not when he could go one step further. "My name's Arthur."

She blinked. "If you tell me that your last name is Pendragon, I'm going to get up and run out of here as fast as I can. Or maybe suggest we start a performance troupe."

He laughed, pleased that her equilibrium had returned. "Actually, it's Davies."

"Oh!" She brightened. "Are you related to Meg Davies? I'm supposed to meet with her at Curiouser & Curiouser...which I think this is, considering all the awesome items on displays I saw out there."

She'd been more shaken than he'd realized. "Meg is my mum," he told her, urging her to drink a bit more water. "I'll ring her to let her know you're here. She usually comes 'round about eleven."

"That's when I'm supposed to meet with her," Morgan said, clutching the glass in both hands. "I didn't realize I'd gotten here so early for my appointment—I thought it would take longer to walk here from the castle. I think I'm still out of sorts from my flight over."

Arthur hid a frown. If she was there to see his mother, that meant she was probably in need of psychic healing. Why his mother didn't tell him about her lovely American visitor, he didn't know. Probably thought he had too much on his plate. Which he did, between running the shop, going on collection excursions, and guarding the astral. He wanted to make time for Morgan, though. He wanted to know more about her, wanted to hear her talk for hours. He wanted to help her, to ease the pain that had her clutching her forehead. He wanted to hold her hand again. "Last night you said you were injured."

"Yes." Her gaze hollowed. "It happened earlier in the fall. I attempted to help local law enforcement find a missing person. I do that by locating them on the astral. I found her and notified the authorities. Unfortunately, her kidnapper wasn't an ordinary human."

He made a guess. "A Shadowling?"

"It must have been in human skin. It attacked both of us, and I failed to defeat it. Failed to protect the girl. The encounter left a mark on my back and shredded my shields. I haven't been able to travel since."

"Until last night?"

She nodded, then frowned. "But I couldn't go back after you kicked me out, so I don't know if traveling's a sign of being on the mend or if it was just a fluke. I also have episodes in which I'm bombarded with all the psychic noise of those around me. It's been...unbearable at times."

It was probably worse than that. "I imagine that's why you're wearing that stone."

"It is." She touched the pendant. "I also have a set of stones to ward my sleep, but sometimes the nightmares still crash through. In fact, the only time that I've truly felt more like myself is when..."

She gestured between them, and he realized what she inferred. "When we touched earlier?"

"Yes." She drank another sip of water, then looked at him, her dark brown eyes flecked with gold and filled with weary and caution. "It might have been a fluke, but do you think...would you mind taking my hand again?"

He didn't mind at all. He also wanted to know if the magic that had flared between them was a momentary quirk or something that they could tap into at will. Wordlessly, he raised his hands, palms facing up. He held still as Morgan extended her hands to surround his. No touching yet, but he could feel her warmth along his skin, warmth he inexplicably very much wanted to get closer to.

As if she'd read his mind, she grasped his hands. Heat, not magic, flooded him. It was an effort to keep his shields in place when everything in him wanted to reach out to her.

"It's strange," she murmured, her voice taking on a dreamy quality. "You're very well shielded, but I can still sense your magic. It's like a pulse. A very powerful pulse. No, a beacon."

She brushed her thumbs over the backs of his hands, and he had to grit his teeth against the sudden bolt of demand that shot through him. He must have shifted or made a noise because she tightened her grip. "Are you all right?"

"Fine," he answered, aware of how husky his voice sounded. He changed his grip so that he held her hands, his thumbs brushing over her soft knuckles in slow, soothing strokes. He had to clear his throat before he spoke. "Do you feel that?"

"Yes." She shivered. "It feels like—you know how you step into the shower, and it's the perfect temperature, and you're just..."

She released a happy sigh. "That's what this feels like."

"That's it exactly." He tried to keep his tone light, but now he had a visual of her taking a shower dancing through his brain. Not the thoughts he should be having of a complete stranger. No, not a stranger, but one who felt like a dear and forgotten friend, one he wanted to acquaint himself with again.

"Okay." She drew in a slow breath, then gazed into his eyes, a warm smile plumping her coppery cheeks. "Would you mind dropping your shields?"

"Not at all. In 3...2...1."

He dropped his shields. Once again, magic flared between them in happy recognition. Then it sputtered and subsided. Her ability was like her voice—warm, honey-like—but it seemed subdued, as if it had been stifled.

No, not stifled. Wounded. He remembered how he'd first seen her during their astral travel, a gilded angel, bright and beautiful, with a dark blotch in the center of her back.

"It's the blot," she whispered into the charged quiet. "After I got injured, I lost most of my ability, my shields were shredded, and I haven't been able to help anybody. It's been hard, but this, this is the best I've felt in weeks. It's nice."

She swallowed hard, then gave him a watery smile. "It's better than nice."

Protectiveness surged inside him. He wanted her to feel better than nice. He wanted to help her heal, help her be whole. He wanted to know what that would feel like.

Power swelled in answer. She sucked in a breath with a soft "oh" of surprise as she shifted in her seat. Perhaps he could help her, focus his extrasense on the Shadow stain, then blast it with Light magic until it was nothing but a distant memory. "I'll help you."

"That's enough."

Chapter Four

"Tell me what happened."

Morgan tamped down the urge to fidget. Mrs. Davies had sent Arthur back to mind the shop while she took Morgan to the flat above, leaving her keenly bereft of his magical support. Not that she could blame the older woman. If some strange Light Adept who'd been attacked by a Shadowling was caught making grabby hands with her son, well, Morgan would be a little upset herself. Nothing untoward had happened between her and Arthur, nothing physical anyway, but she still felt the glide of Arthur's magic along her skin like a lover's touch. Which explained why she was squirming as if Mrs. Davies had caught her doing the horizontal tango with her son.

"I'm an astral traveler. Sometimes I help the authorities find missing people—"

"I already know that." The older woman waved a hand in dismissal. "I'm referring to your interaction with my son."

Morgan winced. Of course she was. Mrs. Davies looked nothing like the plump English witch Morgan had envisioned, a magical Mrs.

Bennett eager to marry her daughters off. Instead, she had a slender build to match her height, a sharp personality to match her gaze, and if she'd said she was a retired assassin, Morgan would have believed her.

"I'm not sure." Which was true, if barely.

Mrs. Davies cocked her head, the silver in her cap of blonde hair glinting in the light, causing Morgan to revise her assessment. Perhaps she was a retired prison warden. "I can sense Arthur's magic on you. He doesn't readily reveal his abilities, so I'm quite interested in knowing what made him do that."

"Well, Mrs. Davies..."

"Meg."

Morgan licked her lips then tried again. "Ms. Meg..."

"Meg," the Light healer retorted. "Call me Meg."

"Ma'am." Morgan curled her hand on her knees. "You know my grandmother. Do you have any idea what she'd do to me if I disrespected an elder in age, experience, and association by calling you by your first name?"

Morgan shuddered. "For all I know, Ma Belle could be listening in right now. Just consider it a quirky southern American thing, but I cannot call you by your first name."

A shadow of amusement bent the elder's lips. "If it makes you comfortable, you may call me Ms. Meg."

"Thank you, ma'am—uhm, Ms. Meg." She'd just have to practice until she could comfortably say it.

Ms. Meg clapped her hands together. "Now that the formalities are over, let's return to the topic at hand. What happened between you and Arthur?"

Morgan knew better than to prevaricate any longer. "I can't shield very well these days," she admitted. "Our magics—I guess they're similar since we're both astral travelers—said hello to each other like greeting old friends."

Surprise crossed Meg's expression. "He told you that he's a traveler?"

"I saw him last night. I spontaneously traveled and met him on the astral. I mistook him for a Light Guardian before I realized he was human like me. Then something roared, making the astral tremble, and Arthur kicked me out. Even though I tried to go back, I couldn't. When I got here today, I was so surprised to see him that I stumbled. He grabbed my hand to steady me, and our magics caused a happy flare, before the world went gloriously quiet and still. We pulled apart, and the world crashed back in."

She blew out a frustrated breath and finished the story. "His magic was comforting to me and pushed away some of the noise I've been dealing with since my extrasense was injured. We were trying to see if he could do it again when you arrived."

"I see."

The ultimate non-committal comment. "I do feel marginally better, so maybe after another good night's sleep, I'll be that much further along."

"Your grandmother told me about your confrontation on the astral," Meg said quietly. "She also told me how you've been struggling since then."

Morgan had done her best to hide her struggle from her family, not wanting to worry them, but obviously, she hadn't done as good a job as she'd hoped. Some days were better than others; the days she didn't awake screaming from nightmares were the best ones. This was the best day she'd had in weeks, and she was terrified that it was a fluke and things would be all downhill from here.

"The matriarch asked you to decide, didn't she?" Morgan asked, realization a cold stone in her gut. "You have to determine whether I'm salvageable or not."

"Morgan." Meg pressed her lips into a flat line before speaking. "Your grandmother sent you here because she knows that I am one of the few Light Adepts who can stop Shadow from spreading and perhaps remove it altogether. If anyone can salvage you, I am the one."

The confidence in the other woman's voice rang a bell of hope in Morgan's chest. "I believe you."

"As you should." Meg flexed her fingers. "Let's see what we're dealing with. Drop your shields."

Morgan slouched down in the plush armchair, drew in a long slow breath then released it and her shields at the same time, leaving herself open to Meg's psychic touch. The pressure in the room increased as the older woman stretched her right hand out just above the crown of Morgan's head. Heat enveloped her, pressing against her aura, Meg's probing touch searching for a way inside. This was different than opening herself to Arthur. Although she tried to loosen up, it wasn't easy, especially knowing that Meg literally held her life in her hands.

"This will go easier and faster if you relax."

"I'm trying."

"Try harder," Meg ordered. "Focus on something that makes you happy."

Morgan closed her eyes and thought about her café. That led to her thinking of the last time she'd been there when Ma Belle and her parents had staged their intervention. She forced herself to ease her grip on the chair. Think of something else, something warm and comforting. Like the perfect cup of tea on a rainy day curled up on the couch, sunlight on her face as she walked the beach on Tybee Island.

The warmth of Arthur's magic surrounding her, easing the cacophony in her head.

She blinked open her eyes as Meg sighed, then asked, "Have you been marked?"

"Yes. It burns on my back."

The healer rose. "May I?"

Morgan reached for the hem of her sweater then leaned forward, pulling the back of the sweater up to her nape. Once again, she felt Ms. Meg's extrasense, just a slight brush of power against the mark. Morgan gasped as a hot needle-prick of pain stabbed her shoulder. The healer's magic immediately retreated, and she gave a light pat on Morgan's shoulder. "Do you mind if I take a picture of it?"

"No, ma'am. Ms. Meg."

Morgan waited as patiently as she could as the other woman used her phone to snap a picture before pulling her sweater back down. "Have you seen something like this before?"

"Not in person," the healer said, returning to her chair. "As I suspected, it's Shadowblight."

"What exactly is that?"

"Think of it as an infection. It feeds on Light magic, your extrasense."

Tension tightened Morgan's muscles. "That doesn't sound good."

"It isn't." Meg rubbed at her forehead. "Have you seen it? The mark on your back?"

"Not since I left the hospital." She hadn't wanted to see it again. Out of sight, out of mind.

The healer didn't ask, simply held up the phone for Morgan to see. "Is it different?"

Morgan's sharp intake of breath sounded loudly in the quiet room. If she hadn't been there, she would have claimed the image a fake.

What had been a half-dollar-sized blotch in the hospital had unfurled and spread into a black-inked vine popping with what looked like flowers. It would have been beautiful as a tattoo but this, this was a deadly monstrosity.

"It's…" Morgan swallowed and tried again. "It's more than doubled."

"I was afraid of that." Meg returned her phone to her pocket. "As a Light Adept, you give it a lot to feed on, and it has the potential to spread throughout your system. If it spreads that far, becoming the Shadowblight itself is a certainty. There will be very little of you left."

"My grandmother wouldn't let it spread that far," Morgan whispered. "She'd call for a Shadowchaser to take care of it, of me. It's happened to the family before."

"I know." So much weight filled Meg's tone that Morgan wondered how much she did know, how Ma Belle had known of this Adept in this tiny English town in the first place.

"Can't you fix it?" Desperation clawed at her insides. "Just blast it with your Light magic or something?"

"Of course," Meg answered, her tone dry. "Why use a candle when a flamethrower is handy? It's not as if you need your heart or your brain, right?"

Morgan pursed her lips. "I concede your point."

"How kind of you," the other woman murmured. "For what it's worth, that is why I stopped your experiment with Arthur. He would have wanted to help. That's his nature. His nature is also to charge right in, sword blazing. The consequences of that wouldn't have been good for either of you."

Arthur's gorgeous blue eyes filled her memory. "I appreciate his kindness, but I don't want him to be hurt because of me. Could this

Shadowblight thing jump from me to him? If you'd rather I avoid him, I will."

"I appreciate the offer, but I don't think that will be necessary. Repairing your shields should be enough to keep the blight from transferring inadvertently. Healing runs in our family, but removing Shadowblight requires a little more finesse. Lucky for you, I have that skill."

"Awesome." Hope surged anew as Morgan settled back in the chair. "Okay, I'm ready."

"So impatient, you Americans," Meg murmured without heat. "I do need you to understand that I won't be able to excise all Shadow from you. As enhanced as we Light Adepts are, we're still human, which means Light and Shadow coexist in all of us to varying degrees."

"I know." It was something all Lafayettes learned when they came into their gifts. "I also know this feels different, like it's gnawing on my insides."

"Which is why I'm going to do everything in my power to remove it from your system." Meg gave the back of her hand a light pat. "First, I'll repair your shields so that you're not as battered psychically. That can be done today. I'm also hoping to create a barrier around the blight to keep it contained. Then we'll work on excising it. I'll need to be careful, so it will take several sessions."

"Good thing I've got nothing else to do for the next two weeks."

"You also need to keep that positive attitude," Meg admonished her. "While the blight can feed on your Light magic, it can also heighten negative thoughts and emotions. The best way to fight that, while we work on cutting it out, is for you to fill your spirit with Light."

"Can I use spirits to fill my spirit?" Morgan quipped.

"Depends. Are you a happy drunk or a mean drunk? And do you want to lower your inhibitions that far?"

"I was joking." There was no way she'd voluntarily give up self-control, and drinking to excess would definitely do that. Even so, she didn't need to be psychic to know that there was definitely a cocktail in her future. Maybe two.

"Joking is good," Meg said with a sharp nod. "Even bad jokes. Shall we begin?"

Morgan blew out a breath. "Ready when you are."

***

Although Arthur had spent most of his time helping holiday shoppers and trying not to think about Morgan upstairs with his mother, the American had consumed his thoughts. He worried about her injury, how it impacted her extrasense, and if it could be reversed. If anyone could heal her shields and expunge the Shadow, his mother was the one. Relief made him smile as he watched her and his mother return to the shop. "How did it go?"

"It was a great start," Morgan answered, returning his smile. "I feel better already, but I know I still have a way to go before I'm firing on all cylinders again."

"We've made progress," Meg Davies said, handing Arthur Morgan's coat. "Follow my instructions, and your recovery will go faster."

"Yes, ma'am."

"Meg."

Arthur winced. He'd been on the receiving end of that tone more than once. Morgan dipped her head. "Yes, Ms. Meg."

Arthur noted that her accent sounded stronger than it had earlier. "It must have been a tiring session."

"It was." She raised the back of her hand to her mouth to stifle a yawn. "Excuse me. It was, but even more so for your mother, I'm sure."

"I'm fine." His mother faced him after he helped Morgan into her coat. "Arthur, will you be a dear and take Morgan back to the castle? She could use a bite to eat as well."

"I don't want to impose..." Morgan began, but his mother cut her off.

"Nonsense. Magical work takes energy and magical healing, even more so. We don't need you passing out in the middle of Castle Road, do we?"

"No, ma—Meg," Morgan replied, then shook her head in wonderment. "You remind me of my grandmother."

"Considering what I know of Belle Lafayette, I'll take that as a compliment." His mother made shooing motions at them. "Off you go. I'll stay to help with the last of our visitors, then close the shop. Morgan, I'll see you tomorrow."

"See you then." He guided her to the shop door. "Are you ready for a bite?"

Morgan rubbed at her belly. "I rarely say no to a good meal."

"Same for me." He glanced at his watch. "Is pub food to your liking? The Boar and Knight is nearby. If you want something more posh, there are more restaurants a couple of streets over."

"The Boar and Knight is fine." She rubbed at her forehead. "I don't usually day drink, but I think today is the perfect day to make an exception."

"The pub it is." He escorted Morgan out of the shop. She and his mother had been upstairs for a couple of hours. It was now close to afternoon tea, but he found himself in want of something stronger than tea as well.

The effect of his encounter with Morgan still lingered like the scent of flowers. Even now, his extrasense reached for hers, making him wonder if she also felt the pull and what it might mean if she did.

She tucked her hand into the crook of his elbow, a move that simultaneously surprised, relaxed, and energized him. When she stopped, he covered her hand with his. "I don't mind."

"Same." She shook her head. "This should feel weird, but it doesn't. On the scale of weird things I've encountered over the last few weeks, this seems refreshingly normal."

"Perhaps it is," he suggested. "As we're both travelers, our extrasense is from the same root. Consider it as our extrasense getting better acquainted."

She considered it, then nodded. "That makes sense. I like the sound of that."

He did, too, more than he probably should. Time to direct the conversation to more stable terrain. "Have you been here before?"

"Not to Shropshire. I've been to London several times, of course, and spent a couple of weeks in Scotland. I'll try not to gawk too much as I wander around."

"Our tourism board would say that gawking is very much allowed. Some version of Caynham-on-Ledwyche has been here since the Middle Ages. There's also an Iron Age hill fort just north of us, standing stones in Mortimer Forest, and beautiful countryside that practically seduces you into wandering for kilometers, though not as much this time of year. And, of course, there's the castle."

"I haven't seen much more than my room and the restaurant in the Great Hall," Morgan admitted. "I didn't dare sleep on the plane over, so I crashed soon after I arrived yesterday. I think that may be why I was able to travel last night. I was too exhausted to be in my head worrying about it."

Protectiveness surged inside him, but he tamped it back down. "Was my mum able to help?"

"Yes. My ability to shield isn't at a hundred percent yet, but there's less noise getting through. I can't tell you how good that feels. I'll know how much your mother repaired my shields when I go to sleep tonight."

He absolutely was not thinking about her nighttime ritual and what she wore to bed. His mother would certainly make him regret those thoughts. "It would be lovely to meet you on the astral again."

"As long as there are no dragons." Her fingers tightened on his arm. "Unfortunately, the rest requires a more delicate touch. Your mother said it will more than likely take several sessions, which means I'll be seeing her tomorrow, and the day after, and the day after that."

Three more days of Morgan walking into his shop. Three more opportunities to see her, to get to know her better. "I know you're probably tired of talking about what happened, but if you have need, I'm happy to lend an ear. I'm a great listener, especially when there's a pint in my hand."

She laughed, a wonderful sound. He'd have to make her laugh again. "I'll believe that when I see it. Speaking of which, if I may invoke my inner toddler, are we there yet?"

"As a matter of fact, we are." He stopped in front of the heavy wood door of the town's oldest pub. The Boar and Knight was his favorite, and not only because it was a five-minute walk from his shop. He enjoyed sitting in its dark interior, unwinding while idly listening to some of the elder locals discussing their neighbors' business.

"Welcome to the Boar and Knight."

Chapter Five

- -

The pub was exactly as Morgan had imagined it would be: dark wood and dim lighting, wooden tables and chairs that were likely older than her grandmother. History breathed from every corner, from wood and plaster and leather and vinyl, telling its story in slow, ponderous tones.

Arthur guided her to one of the few booths tucked against one wall, waving a greeting to some of the patrons. Morgan wasn't sure what time it was, but it seemed as if they'd caught the pre-dinner lull. They'd be able to carry on a conversation without yelling. Given the likely nature of their talk, that was a good thing.

"Is this one of those places where everybody knows your name?" she asked, shimmying out of her coat before sliding onto the bench.

"Erm..." Arthur blinked at her for a moment before replying. "I suppose it is. This time of year, we're brimming with tourists who come for the Christmas at the Castle festivities, but being a busy bachelor, I stop in here several times a week for dinner. It's easier than cooking for one and I can better spend that time hunting down new pieces for the shop or fulfilling client requests."

She accepted the menu he handed her, then leaned forward, curious to know more. "Do you spend any time with your parents?"

"It's just my mum. My father's been gone about five years now, and I stopped traveling as much to manage the shop."

"I'm so sorry." She reached out to take his hand, something that was quickly becoming second nature. Meg had done excellent work repairing her shields. Instead of his extrasense, all Morgan felt was the warmth and strength of Arthur's fingers, which she freely admitted, was just as wonderful.

"Thank you." He squeezed her hand. "He went as happily as the cancer would allow and made sure there was an abundance of smiles and good stories to remember him by."

"That's wonderful. Is it just you and your mother then?"

"My sister lives in South Africa with her husband and two boys. Mom has a gentleman friend and a group of friends she calls her coven, although I'm not sure how many of them have any measurable degree of extrasense."

She noticed that he hadn't mentioned anything that he did, so she asked him. "What about you? What do you do when you're not in the shop or traveling the astral helping damsels in distress?"

He leaned forward, tightening his grip on her hand. "For the record, I don't think of you as a damsel in distress, but I'm more than happy to help you in whatever way you need."

Whew. She wasn't sure how he meant his words, but she knew how she took them—straight to her lady parts. *Well, hello there.*

He brushed his thumb along her knuckles, sending sparks flying through her system. Whether it was magical or something much more carnal, she didn't know. She forced herself to look into his eyes and focus on his words. "Most of the time I leave the shop to the staff to travel across Europe hunting for inventory. I'll also take commissions from clients looking for specific items."

His eyes gleamed as he leaned forward again. "I enjoy the thrill of the hunt and the satisfaction of claiming my prize."

Oh, my. She licked her lips as she wondered what it would be like if they hooked up, especially if she had full control of her extrasense. If their initial encounter was any indication...Lord, she hoped he couldn't read her mind. "You sound like a treasure hunter."

"Given the value of some of the pieces I procure, I suppose you could say that I do hunt treasure." He sat back, picking up his menu. "I think I've bored you with my exploits long enough. I should give you a chance to look over the menu."

Picking up hers, she tried not to miss the simple pleasure of holding his hand. She decided to try a little flirting of her own. "I doubt there's anything boring about you, Arthur Davies."

"Thank you." His warm smile sent a slow heat over her. "I shall endeavor to live up to that belief."

She was saved from coming up with a witty reply by the approach of a server. Torn between the cod battered with a local brew and the bangers made of local sausage served with homemade Shropshire blue cheese mashed potatoes, she sighed. "Everything looks so good that I'm just going to have to come back every day until I've eaten around the menu. I'll start with the beer-battered cod, and to drink, I think I'd like to try that Caynham Honey Ale."

"Excellent choice." The server turned to Arthur. "Do you want your usual today?"

"I think so." He handed the menus over. "Thanks, Jimmy."

"What's your usual?" Morgan asked as their server left.

"Gammon steak."

She frowned, trying to remember if she'd seen that on the menu. "What's gammon steak?"

He shook his head with a teasing grin. "I think I'll keep you in suspense for a while longer. Now tell me about you. What do you do when you're not visiting castles on holiday?"

"I own a small tea shop in the southeast part of the States in Savannah, Georgia, called Lafayette's Teas & Reads. We serve the usual café fare, but our specialty is creating custom tea blends for our customers. A couple of times a day we have a tasseography ceremony by appointment in which we serve a proprietary blend in a quiet setting and then read the tea leaves left in the bottom of the cup. We also take appointments for that service."

His eyebrows arched in surprise. "You're public with your abilities?"

The server arrived with their drinks, two dark gold ales in tall, frosty glasses. She took an experimental sip, then a larger one, smacking her lips in satisfaction. "Ah, that hits the spot! To answer your question, there are maybe a couple of hundred Lafayette kinfolk scattered about the southern United States, and we're known for our gifts. My grandmother is the current matriarch, and she manages the family's concerns out of Lafayette House. I would say that most of the family has extrasense to some degree or other, and some others have been able to develop their abilities with practice. We help law enforcement across the country, and some of us use our extrasense in our careers to spread Light as needed. We're as out as we can be."

She took another sip of the damn good ale. "What about you? Are you and your mother out with your abilities?"

He grimaced into his glass. "I'm not. Mum is. My father didn't have a magical bone in his body, but he loved my mother to bits and supported both of us in exercising our talents. Unfortunately, I haven't been able to find someone for myself with the same disposition."

"I understand." She reached out for his hand again. It should have been weird to want to hold hands with someone she'd only known for a few hours, but with his comfort, warmth, and extrasense calling to her, their connection was undeniable. She just didn't know what to do about it. Well, she had an idea, but it was a wildly inappropriate one.

"My ex-husband thought he knew what he was getting into when we got married. I tried to prepare him, but even though he'd met my parents, grandmother, and a plethora of cousins, he couldn't cope with the reality of marrying into a magical family."

She sighed, pushing old memories away. "So now I'm a thirty-two-year-old divorcee focused entirely on making my little business the best metaphysical café in town, being a doting aunt, and repairing my abilities so that I can actually do my job and help people again."

He raised his glass, his expression a fluid mixture of concern, protectiveness, and appreciation. "Here's to better days."

Considering how awesome this day was going so far, it was almost greedy to want more. Still, she dutifully clinked the rim of her glass against his. "To better days."

Soon after their food arrived, her fish and chips and his gammon steak, which turned out to be a thick ham steak with a fried egg on top and chips on the side. She made a note to try that on a return trip, then wondered if the pub had hot sauce on hand. Too bad she hadn't tucked any into her purse, but she hadn't been thinking about food when packing for the trip.

"If you like, I would be happy to show you the sights of Caynham-on-Ledwyche," he offered as she liberally doused her fish with malt vinegar. "Most of the attractions around town and the castle are best on foot. In fact, the standing stones in Mortimer Forest are a field away from my mother's house. If we finish our meal in time, we can walk to the site and return before night sets in."

"Visiting the standing stones sounds great, but I don't want to take you away from your shop during prime retail season," she protested. It was a half-hearted protest, made only because she was raised to be polite.

"My staff would tell you that I'm in the way, and they're glad to be rid of me," he answered with a self-deprecating laugh. "Besides, it's a pleasure to spend time with you, Morgan."

"You make think differently when we're done," she joked. "I have no qualms about enjoying my food."

Suiting words to action, Morgan dug into her food, savoring the carb-y goodness of the potatoes and the battered fish. Mostly, she enjoyed Arthur's company, the quiet moments as they ate, and the engaging moments in which they discussed the must-see sights around town. After months of seeing the dour faces of her relatives as she wrestled with her psychic and physical injuries, it was a wonderful change of pace to meet another magic user who didn't think she was days away from being collected by a Shadowchaser, never to be seen again. It didn't hurt that said magic user was gorgeous either, with a smile at times welcoming, teasing, and sensual with eyes full of acceptance and invitation.

She wanted to accept that invitation, wanted to explore the possibilities that their extrasense encounter had only hinted at. The need coursed through her like hunger demanding to be sated. And yet a part of her wondered, was it her libido making the demand or something darker?

His voice cut into her suddenly morose thoughts. "What are you thinking about that has you frowning so deeply?"

"I have a question I want to ask you about last night." She lowered her voice. "That thing that you were standing guard against. Do you know what it is?"

"No." He reached for his ale, clearly thinking. "When I'm on the astral, I spend my time around town or in the center of the standing stones or meditating on the akashic records. There have been a handful of confrontations with Shadowlings, but once I don my Light armor, they usually scatter."

He fiddled with his glass, disquiet filling his gaze. "The presence from last night, I first became aware of it a week ago. It's stronger and darker than anything I've encountered before, but so far, it's remained on the periphery."

She bit her bottom lip. "You don't think it will for much longer, do you?"

"I don't."

"Is that why you kicked me off the astral? How did you do that, by the way?"

"I created a doorway to a lower plane and shoved you through," he admitted. "I do apologize for the abruptness of it, but I feared you might be in danger."

She bristled immediately. "And you weren't? What if you had been attacked after I left? I could have helped you!"

He stared at her in surprise before his cheeks reddened. "I apologize again," he said, his voice quiet. "It's been some time since I've had someone not related to me wanting to watch my back, and never one who could also travel."

Once again, their hands tangled. "I understand." How could she not? She had a wide network of relatives, but nearly all of her friends were cousins. After being burned by her ex, she was cautious with people wanting to get close to her because of her name and her abilities.

After her failure to save Penny, she was cautious about her extrasense, period.

"It's probably for the best," she said with a sigh. "My magic isn't exactly reliable these days. What happened after I left?"

"Nothing." He looked up at her disbelieving snort. "Honestly. The presence retreated, then faded. It was as if a storm coalesced on the horizon, then dissipated."

"Do you think it's gone for good?"

He shook his head. "I think it's waiting. For what, I have no idea. Perhaps it's gaining strength, waiting for the right time."

"The right time to what?" Morgan asked, suppressing a shiver.

"I wish I knew." Storm clouds gathered in his eyes. "I don't know what type of Shadowling it is, and I don't know anything else about it other than the fact that it can travel on the astral. I don't know if it exists only on the astral or if it has a physical body nearby. It's not as if there's a wiki of Shadow creatures."

"Not one us mere mortals can access, you mean." Bitterness coated her tongue, prompting her to drain the remainder of her ale. "I bet those Shadowchasers know every kind of Shadowling out there since it's their job to stop them. Or so I've heard."

Arthur gave her a measuring look. "You sound skeptical."

"Jaded, maybe." She gave him a brief rundown of her cousin Laney's encounter with a Shadowchaser, and how her dad became a director. "Even with my dad as a director, I wouldn't be surprised if the organization that manages the Chasers has a dossier on the Lafayette clan. They already know about my problem."

Concern lit his eyes. "Do you consider yourself at the same stage that your cousin was when the Shadowchaser was called?"

"No." She shook her head to emphasize her point. "My grandmother wouldn't have sent me here on my own if that were true. She knows how to contact the Shadowchaser for our area, but I don't, and I don't care to learn."

"Why not?"

"Because from what I heard, Shadowchasers are the final solution. Gilead agents capture, but Chasers kill. I've heard enough about the one monitoring the supernatural community up in Atlanta to know she doesn't sound like someone I want to meet. I need to get this blight removed before a Shadowchaser is summoned to remove me."

"Then trust my mother and your grandmother," Arthur urged. "Trust me. We'll help you. I swear, we'll do everything we can to remove this blight."

She dropped her gaze to the table, hoping Arthur hadn't seen the desperate hope that had flared to life, returning again and again, a phoenix full of her wishes, prayers, and dreams. That desperate hope, fueled by his certainty and his mother's skills, burned her fear and despair to embers.

"Morgan." He sandwiched her hand between both of his. "Look at me."

She did and immediately became lost in that piercing blue gaze and the fire burning within. The weight of his stare and the softness of his extrasense brushed against her as gently and as profoundly as his thumb along her pulse, leaving her to wonder if that fire in his gaze was more sensual than righteous. If just his thumb brushing her wrist could evoke this type of response in her, what would happen with a simple hug or a not-so-simple kiss?

"Come back."

The soft command brought her back to her senses. She blinked, forcing herself to focus on his face and not the sensation unfurling low in her belly. "Yes?"

He drew in a breath. "I should probably stop touching you like this, but I find it nearly impossible to move away."

"Did I ask you to stop?" Why was her tone so breathy? She knew why.

"No, and that's the only reason why I don't consider this to be bad manners." Another one of those deep glances. "So, have you made any plans for your free time besides recuperating from my mother's healing sessions?"

"I thought about being an actual tourist," she confessed. "You probably know already that there's a massive setup on the castle grounds that I'd like to visit, and of course, you already mentioned the standing stones."

"Does that mean you agree to have me as your tour guide?"

It was time to ask the question she should have asked the moment they had sat down. "I'm not taking your time away from someone else, am I?"

"I suppose I didn't make myself clear earlier." His grip tightened. "I'm not seeing anyone. Is there someone waiting for you back home?"

She rapidly shook her head. "No. No one, not even a prospect. Does that mean I'll get to see more of your bad manners?"

A dangerous smile bowed his lips. "Whatever you want, consider me willing."

Suddenly, her sweater felt too hot and too tight. She grabbed her ale and swallowed down the remainder. "Duly and definitely noted. Right now, I'd like another round and some dessert. It's been a long time since I've been in this good of a mood, and I have you to thank."

"It's my pleasure."

Morgan breathed in slowly and deeply as Arthur turned to signal their server. There was no doubt that the flirty desire was mutual. Whatever it was that was developing between them, she wanted to see where it would go and how far. If it was just a way to distract herself from her Shadow problem, she believed he wouldn't mind. If it was on the way to being something more, she believed he wouldn't mind that either.

Chapter Six

"What do you think of her?"

Arthur had expected his mother to call him before he had the chance to call her, but he hadn't expected her to ring as soon as he crossed the threshold. "I won't bother to ask how you know I'm home. Mind if I remove my coat before the interrogation begins?"

"Think of it as a debrief rather than an interrogation," his mother suggested. "You spent a significant amount of time with Morgan today. And she seemed at ease with you. I'd like to know your opinion of her."

"I think she's lovely," he replied, keeping his tone casual as he stowed his coat. He thought her much more than that. "She's friendly, smart, and funny, which is amazing considering what she's been through."

"She told you?"

He wondered at the surprise in his mother's words. "Not every minute detail, but enough. I know she tried to help find someone by locating them on the astral plane, got trapped there, and earned battered shields and a taint of Shadow for her trouble."

"It's more than a taint." She sat down with a heavy sigh. "A taint would fade in time, especially by focusing on positive things that can fill you with Light. This is Shadowblight, a parasite that feeds on Light magic."

Alarm klaxoned inside him, bunching his muscles with the urge to do something. "It's been eating at her magic for weeks?"

His mother nodded. "Poor Morgan's been fighting it as best she can with her family's help, but it's growing. If I can't remove it, it will consume her."

"You can't allow that to happen." His fingernails dug into his palms as he imagined Morgan without her magic, with her Light extinguished, her soul devoured by Shadow. "We can't allow that to happen. She's afraid of Shadowchasers. If one has to be sent after her..."

"Arthur." Caution colored his mother's tone. "I know you want to help her, but you must be careful."

"Careful?" He frowned, astonished at her words. "Morgan wouldn't hurt me!"

"At the moment, I'm more worried about you hurting her than her hurting you."

Astonishment ratcheted higher. "What? Why?"

"Son." That one word held a world of reproach. "You have always been a knight in need of a princess to save. I love that you want to help people, Morgan especially. Perhaps you even need to help. What I fear is that that need could endanger both of you."

"Mostly her, you mean." He locked his jaw to avoid saying more, but he didn't have to. His parents had been there after Callista, helping him stitch the tatters of his life back together. He'd over-compensated by traveling the world searching for artifacts and trinkets to stock the shop, building professional contacts but never getting close to anyone again. Sure, it was a lonely existence at times, but it was better than the alternative, the choice Callista had made despite his every effort to help.

"I am well aware of my limitations," he finally said, bitterness sour on his tongue. "I'm not a healer. I'll never be a healer, and I can't save everyone."

"Son."

"Do you want me to stay away from her?" he demanded, his hands shaking from being so tightly clenched. "Is that why you're telling me this?"

She snorted. "Morgan asked the same question."

He stilled. "What did you tell her?"

"Considering that you've spent the better part of a day with her, what do you think I said?"

He dropped into a chair, relief unhinging his knees. If his mother had asked him to stay away from Morgan, he would have tried. He also knew he would have failed miserably. "We have a connection. We're fellow travelers, kindred spirits. I don't know how else to explain it."

"You don't have to explain it to me. I had a strong connection with your father. While he didn't have extrasense, he said that he knew we were meant to be from the moment we met. I knew it too, but I fought it for six months." She sighed. "Six wasted months."

Her sadness pulled at him. His parents' relationship was the stuff of legends, a goal he'd given up on ever achieving for himself. Now, suddenly, those thoughts were back, thanks to Morgan. Yes, as irrational as that was to think about someone he'd known for less than a day, he'd spent the short journey back from the castle considering the possibilities. He had no idea if Morgan felt their connection as strongly as he did or if she would be open to exploring the potential of more. Add in the fact that she had a full life an ocean away, and he had to wonder if he'd finally, truly lost his senses.

"You'll be able to heal her, won't you? What happens if you aren't able to heal her?"

"Are you doubting my skills?"

"I have absolute faith in your ability. The fact that Morgan is here means that she and her family do too. I simply want to know what's the worst that could happen."

His mother sighed again. "If I fail, the Shadowblight wins, and Morgan loses. I will have to call her grandmother and have a conversation that I haven't had in more than twenty years. I do not want to do that to Belle Lafayette again, and I certainly do not want to do that to Morgan. I will not fail."

The conviction in his mother's voice sat on him like Sisyphus' stone. He knew she would do everything in her power to save Morgan. So would he.

If his mother couldn't heal Morgan, there was someone else he knew who could possibly help. Someone who wasn't afraid of working outside the system and using unorthodox methods. He already had a meeting scheduled in two days regarding an artifact that had come into his possession. It would be a simple thing to mention Morgan's issue and ask for help. He just had to hope Morgan wouldn't hate the idea—and him.

***

Later, Arthur lay in bed, staring up at the ceiling. He was reasonably sure that enough time had passed for Morgan to be asleep already. If not, he'd visit after his usual astral rounds. Even if she couldn't travel, they could probably dream-speak if she wanted.

Excitement over possibly seeing her on the astral warred with the need to center himself so that he could project. Closing his eyes, he breathed deeply in and then just as deeply out, focusing his attention on the physicality of breathing. Slowly, he used his outward breaths to relax each part of his body in turn: head, shoulders, each arm, torso, and each leg. Breathing deeply, feeling lighter with each breath.

Fly.

His astral body rose up from his physical form and into the night sky. Nothing beat that first rush of being free of his corporeal body. A wave rippled through the atmosphere, transporting him to what he called the first floor, the dreaming world. He noticed that a few of the villagers were in the midst of flying dreams. They had the potential to become astral travelers, but he had yet to discover anyone who had taken that next step.

Which was why encountering Morgan had been so miraculous. It had taken a monumental act of willpower to refrain from peppering her with questions. He had to remind himself that he'd only known her for one day; he didn't need to be over-eager and scare her off. Yet here he was on the astral, hoping to catch a glimpse of Morgan or her dreams.

Thought became action, and he found himself hovering outside Morgan's hotel room window. Not wanting to be a Peeping Tom, he rose to the initial astral plane. Everything on the dream plane that had been near exact replicas of the waking world now transformed into energy outlines. Both living and inanimate objects glowed with neon-like auras, especially the centuries-old castle and its grounds.

With structures merely an idea, he could clearly see the energies of every person in the hotel. He identified Morgan by the powerful resonance of a protective crystal array that covered every corner of her room. Nothing would be able to breach the Light barrier. If this was the strength of her extrasense stained by Shadow, how powerful would she be with the taint removed?

"Arthur."

Energy vibrated as Morgan called his name. Her astral self sat up. As she turned to him, her astral form solidified into her waking world visage. Although his astral body technically didn't possess a heart, he nonetheless felt a jump when she smiled at him.

"It's me," he finally answered. "Would you like to travel with me?"

"I would love to, but I can't seem to leave my body."

Disappointment swamped him, immediately chased by inspiration. "I think I can help with that. May I come in?"

"Sure."

She made a lowering gesture, and one portion of the barrier slid down, allowing him entry. He moved beside her. "Let's try this. You concentrate on rising free, and I'll focus on pulling you out. I think it will work."

"Okay." She closed her eyes to concentrate, then reached for his hand. As before, magic flared the moment they touched, a supernova compared to the waking world. He would swear that he heard and felt a click as their extrasense met like a reunion of old friends, and something settled happily in his spirit.

With a gentle tug, he pulled her astral body free of her corporeal form. A delighted laugh pealed out a heartbeat before she threw her arms around his neck, pressing her astral body fully against his. "Thank you!"

Surprise jackknifed through him, immobilizing him as her extrasense unfurled to cocoon them in soft, gold-white energy as sweet as a spring sun. He had enough wits about him to note that he couldn't see any sign of a mark on her. Was it because their extrasense had merged? Was it—

She rubbed her cheek against his collarbone. "This feels good, like a favorite blanket."

Before he could react to her words or her gesture, she pulled away. "Sorry for overstepping, but I—oomph!"

Arthur grabbed her, pulled her close, and caged her in his arms. "Not overstepping, and I agree with you. Let's stay like this for a little while longer."

They did, floating free of the hotel walls. Her arms tightened around his waist, her cheek resting against his shoulder. He held her just as tightly, loath to let her go. Their extrasense purred like a contented kitten, sweetness and warmth soothing his soul.

It would be too easy to become addicted to this sensation, to magically connect with her. He had to remind himself that she needed healing, that she was a foreigner who'd soon return home. He also reminded himself that his mother was an excellent healer, and that time and distance meant nothing on the astral plane. That he'd forever regret letting Morgan go without at least trying for more.

He eased his hold. She stepped back, then held out her hand. "My extrasense already misses yours," she explained. "Besides, you have to safely escort me back to my body, right?"

"We should be safe on this level," he assured her, entwining his fingers with hers. "Shall I take you on a tour?"

"I'd like that."

They rose until the entirety of the castle grounds filled their vision. "Caynham castle has been here for nearly a thousand years," he explained, "so it's had centuries of absorbing magic."

"I noticed it yesterday," Morgan said, then laughed. "Was it only yesterday? It's very ancient magic here, different from what I feel back home on River Street. Maybe it's because the Savannah River's been engineered away from its original flow. Then again, it's a river, so of course, it's always changing. Why am I rambling?"

"If I had to guess, it's because you're excited about traveling again? Do you pull your power from the river?" he asked as they crossed Ledwyche Brook.

"Sometimes. But there's power in being a Lafayette, and there's enough of us in the region that we have our own power network. Only a few of us can tap into it at will—my grandmother as the matriarch, my father as the incoming patriarch, and a handful of other elders."

She stopped, wrapping her arms about herself as if to ward off a chill that couldn't be felt on the astral. "If I had been able to reach the collective, I might have been able to save Penny. And myself."

Bitterness and remorse saturated the air between them, an emotional fog. He knew all too well how easy it was to get lost in it, how difficult it was to find your way back out again. "Three years ago, I tried to save someone. I couldn't. I know how that guilt and grief never really goes away. Neither does the anger."

"The anger." She huffed, balling her hands as thunder rumbled in the plane above them. "My therapist didn't warn me about it. How it's like a sneak attack that you're completely defenseless against. How insidious—"

She broke off, then gathered herself. "You know what? I don't want to talk about this anymore. Show me something else."

If it was a distraction she wanted, he'd be happy to provide one. "Let me take you to one of my favorite places."

Between one blink and the next, they arrived. "This is Mortimer Forest, and in the center is a group of standing stones."

"Whoa."

The standing stones, the site of thousands of rituals over thousands of years, pulsed with waves of light, some cool blue-white, some warm yellow-white. Light and Shadow cohabitated there, one thriving by the longest day, the other by the longest night.

"It's strange," Morgan murmured as she surveyed the stones. "Light and Shadow seem to coexist here and the land is healthy, happy even. I wonder why it can't be the same inside me."

Good question. "Maybe what infected you isn't trying to coexist."

"That would explain why it's fighting your mother so fiercely."

He wanted to offer her reassurance, but words weren't enough. Instead, he turned her away from the forest and toward the field. "Look."

"That's a huge source of extrasense there. It feels familiar. Wait." She turned to him. "Is that...your mother?"

"It is. That cottage has belonged to us for a few generations—or, as my grandmother had put it, our family belongs to it and the land. You can see lines of energy running from the forest and the stones across the field. Mum draws on that energy when she needs to, like when she's doing healing work."

"The magic here is amazing. Your mother must feel supercharged when she taps into this." She stretched a hand toward the stones. "I'd like to visit them in the waking world, if we could."

"Of course." As if he could refuse anything she'd ask of him. "I spent a lot of time playing in the forest and at the standing stones. In fact, I traveled for the first time as a boy while inside the circle. I thought I was dreaming. Mum thought she'd seen my ghost. Her being scared, scared me back into my body, and I ran home to tell her what happened. That's how I learned what astral traveling is."

"My first experience was something like that," she confessed. "Luckily, my father realized what happened and brought me back to my body. Daddy-daughter time became training sessions with a trip for ice cream afterward."

"I've learned by trial and error. Astral travelers must be few and far between."

"I tell you what." She squeezed his arm in excitement. "I'll ask my dad to meet us on the astral tomorrow. I bet the both of you can share some stories. He says time and distance don't mean much on the astral, so we should be able to easily connect with him. I think you'll hit it off."

"I'd appreciate talking to a traveler with his experience," Arthur said, ignoring the little hop in his gut at the thought of meeting her father. He dearly wanted to make a good impression on Mr. Lafayette not only as a fellow traveler, but also as a person.

"We should probably head back," he suggested. "Mum's getting her rest. We should do the same."

"All right." Morgan sighed. "I really don't want our date to end."

"Date?"

"Isn't it?" She looked over her shoulder at him. "You aren't thinking what I'm thinking. Well damn. I was hoping tomorrow we'd have another one."

"Tomorrow we will absolutely have a date. And the day after that. We'll date every day that you're here. And since time and distance don't mean much, I'm even going to date you on the astral."

Her smile was a sunrise of encouragement. "I like the way you think, Arthur Davies."

Chapter Seven

C OME UPSTAIRS.

The two-word text stabbed a bolt of fear deep into Arthur's gut. He raced for the stairs, taking them two at a time. *Please let them be all right.*

He headed for the spare bedroom, skidding to a stop in the doorway. Morgan lay on the bed, her face scrunched with effort, sweat beading on her brow. His mother sat in a chair beside her, slouched over, a trembling hand on Morgan's back. Both women looked as if they'd topple over at any moment.

He gripped his mother's shoulders, pulling her away from Morgan. "What happened?"

"I was careless." She clutched his forearms for support. "I thought we'd made progress with the last two days of sessions, but this thing is stubborn. I thought to pull more power to push it out. It-it retaliated by attacking both of us, especially Morgan. I believe she's trapped in a lucid dream or stuck on the astral plane. I can't wake her, and I can't draw her back."

"How long?"

"Longer than I'm comfortable with. She's hurting."

Morgan's pained whimper tore at him. Icy fingers of fear slid along his skin as he fell to his knees beside the bed. He gathered her hand in his. Their connection ignited then immediately banked, as if something was trying to extinguish it. His gut clenched. The dimness of her extrasense compared to when they'd first met was striking. He felt the weight of time pressing down on him but resolutely shook it off. It wasn't too late. "I'll bring her back."

"Be careful, son."

Morgan was trapped, being consumed by Shadowblight. He'd be as careful as he could for her sake. He'd also go in sword swinging, again for her sake. He wasn't going to lose her like this. He would bring her back. He had to.

Resting his forehead against their intertwined hands, he closed his eyes, drew in a slow breath, then reached for the astral. Urgency gripped him, making it difficult to find the calm needed to push free of his body. It took longer than he'd hoped, but he finally pushed free of his body. He aimed for the astral, driven by the need to find Morgan and bring her back. Inky blackness greeted him, with waves of energy arcing around him like a psychic aurora borealis. Morgan was nowhere to be seen.

Holding still, he focused on her, her smile, the sparkle in her eyes, her extrasense. *Morgan, where are you? Help me find you.*

He felt a tug, not from the astral, but from a lower plane—the plane of lucid dreams and nightmares. Forming his shields into armor, he drew his sword and plunged forward.

*****

"Help me!"

The call, desperate, young, and frightened, pulled Morgan like a lodestone. She focused on the call, flying along the astral plane, compelled by the urgent need to answer the call.

FIND HER.

Waves of energy buffeted her, stronger than she'd ever encountered. A storm of evil, gathering strength, deadly and familiar. This wasn't the astral. This was something worse.

God, no.

The nightmare locked onto her, trapping her. Her heart pounded as adrenaline flooded her system, her fight or flight instinct pegging hard to flight. She knew how this ended, and she wanted no part of it.

Wake up, dammit. You've got to wake up!

"Help! Somebody, please help me. He's coming back!"

Morgan picked up speed. Even though she knew this was a dream, it didn't feel like it. Instead, it felt as if she was reliving the tortuous time she'd lost Penny when she'd been attacked. No matter how much she fought to free herself, she was trapped. She was on the astral plane. She could hear Penny calling for help. Could feel the evil amassing, ready to rip the poor girl to shreds. Ready to rip *her* to shreds.

Not this time, not if she could help it.

Penny's energy rippled across the astral, and suddenly Morgan was there. She saw the girl's astral form, a shimmering blue-white fairy with glittering wings. "Hi, Penny,"

The girl stared at her with wide eyes iridescent with fear. "Are you an angel? Am I dead?"

Morgan swallowed the lump in her throat. The nightmare would barrel toward its inevitable catastrophic conclusion, but she still wanted to change the outcome. Still wanted to try. "I'm not an angel. My name is Morgan. I've been looking for you."

"Are you real? This isn't a dream?"

"Yes and no. This is the astral plane. Your subconscious brought you here and that's how I was able to find you. But now I need to find you in the waking world. Do you know where you are, where you were taken?"

"I-I don't know. It was always dark and smelly, and I could hear running water." The child's expression crumpled. "I'm scared."

"I know, sweetheart. It's okay to be scared. But I'm here with you." She took the girl's hand. Her magic, untamed and unfocused, swamped Morgan with frenzied terror. "Focus on your breathing, deep breath in, deep breath out. Good."

She held on with grim determination, calming the girl's wild talent and her panic. "Okay, Penny, here's what we need to do. You see this cord? It's attached to your back. It connects you to your physical body. We're going to follow the cord back so that I can see where you are. Once I know that, I'll go back to my body so that I can tell the police where to find you."

Penny clutched at her. "What if he comes back?"

"We'll find you before he does," Morgan promised, because that was what she'd said back then. She'd been so confident that they would reach Penny in time, rescue her, and catch her kidnapper. None of them had known what sort of monster they would be facing. The fact that she hadn't known, hadn't prepared, was a permanent mark on her psyche.

They traveled, following Penny's cord back down to the physical plane. As before, Morgan noted the dilapidated barn, the creek flowing next to it, the state road roughly two miles west—and the battered covered truck bumping over the rough ground, heading for the barn.

Fear cramped her. "Penny, I have to go. I have to go tell the police where you are."

"No!" The girl latched onto her with a grip almost preternaturally strong. "Please! Don't leave me alone. The bad man will come back! I know he will."

Morgan knew it, too. It would take the police at least an hour to get to the abandoned barn, and by then, it would be too late. "That's why I have to get the police to come here. I can't help you like this, with my astral body. I'll come back as soon as I can."

She tried to leave, to return to the private room at the precinct where her father waited with her physical body and a detective. She'd stayed longer on the astral than she should have; if she stayed much longer, it would become more difficult to leave, and her father would have to drag her back to her body, an action that was sure to be painful for them both.

Penny refused to let go, and Morgan didn't want to use force to extricate herself. The girl was frightened, and rightfully so. She didn't want to leave her, especially knowing what was about to happen.

"All right," she decided. "Come with me. We'll go report to the police and then come back—"

The barn door crashed open. Silhouetted against the doorway was a hulking, man-shaped form. The evil pouring off it in malevolent waves was unlike anything Morgan had experienced before. One word consumed her thoughts.

Run.

Holding tight to Penny, Morgan flew higher into the astral. The creature roared, a trumpeting noise, then followed, transforming into a hulking black shape, blacker than a starless night. Dragon-like, it stretched its claws toward Penny's fairy form.

The young girl shrieked as the creature swiped at her, ripping into her astral body. Anguish buffeted Morgan, a psychic reverb punching holes into her shields. Kicking and screaming, she tried to fight off the beast, tried to protect Penny, protect herself even though she knew it was futile.

Penny's shrieks cut off. Morgan didn't look. She didn't have to; the images had been seared into her memory months before. Penny had been attacked and once again, Morgan had been unable to save her. Once again, she would be attacked next.

Desperate to escape the inescapable, Morgan tried to push through the barrier separating the dreaming and waking worlds. Claws raked at her back. The astral grayed out as pain stabbed at her. An impotent scream rose within her, a desperate, futile call for someone, anyone, to help. No one was going to come. No one was going to save her, not even herself.

A blinding flash of blue-white light sliced through space, darkened by despair. She hunched down and covered her ears as an agonized roar battered at her, a sound she couldn't recall from the real experience. She couldn't understand what this new turn meant. Was she falling deeper into the lucid dreaming plane? Was she going to be trapped within a new hellscape?

"Morgan!"

She froze, then blinked in disbelief. "Arthur?"

He stood before her, a literal knight in shining armor, his sword blazing, driving away the final shards of the nightmare that was more than a dream. She straightened, hope unfurling in her chest. "Is it really you? Are you really here?"

"Yes." He sheathed his sword then reached for her. "Are you all right?"

She danced back. He didn't know how much she wanted to say yes, how much she wanted to touch him to prove that he was real. She did neither. "I knew it was a dream, but it felt different, so I tried. I tried to change things. I tried to save her, escape with her. I tried to fight. I tried."

"I know." Sorrow drenched his features. "I saw. That thing...it's the same thing I've been protecting the town against."

Shock rippled across the plane. That wasn't true. It couldn't be true. "Impossible."

"Is it? Time and space don't mean anything on this plane or the astral. It sounds and feels the same as the entity I encountered."

She didn't know enough about the blight or the thing that killed Penny to be certain of anything. Was it after Arthur because he was also a traveler because she hadn't been able to travel for a while? Would he have been attacked if his shielding wasn't stronger than hers?

She could still feel the burn of claws on her back. Maybe the Shadowblight and Arthur's dragon were one and the same. Mimicking calm to the best of her ability, she turned her back to him. "What does it look like?"

His sharp inhale told her everything she needed to know before his words confirmed it. "There are new tendrils going down your spine to your waist. I'm sorry I was too late to keep it from attacking you."

Too late. The words rang a bell of doom in her soul. It was too late for Penny, and now it was too late for her. Still, she wanted him to know that she'd tried. "I tried to leave. As soon as I realized what this was and what was about to happen...but I couldn't."

Again, he reached out to her, and again, she stepped back, folding her arms across her chest. She wanted his touch, craved it, but she didn't trust herself or the Shadowblight encroaching on her senses. "I can't. I don't trust that I won't hurt you, that this won't infect you, too."

"Morgan, please." Pain dimmed his gaze. "My shields are strong, and I trust you. And I-I need to hold you for my own selfish reasons."

She couldn't deny him, couldn't deny herself. Stepping into his arms, even on the astral, felt like heaven. Probably as close as she'd get now.

He wrapped his arms tight around her, a protective cocoon she desperately needed. "Let me take you back."

Her eyes slid closed. There was so much more she wanted to tell him, this man she'd known for a handful of days yet had connected to so profoundly. Confessions she wanted to make, promises she wanted to give, dreams she wanted to dream. Instead, she settled on one cold, hard truth.

"It would be better to leave me here."

"No."

"The blight is spreading." She stepped back from him. "I know you see it. If I have another nightmare—"

"So we're just supposed to give up?" He shuddered, his eyes wild. "I can't do that. I can't leave you here with that thing. Don't ask that of me."

He was right, it was a horrible thing to ask of him. Besides, she wanted the chance to say goodbye properly to her parents and grandmother. She'd return to the hotel, make videos to send to her parents, and then call her grandmother. Maybe she'd get to meet a Shadowchaser after all.

"All right." She clasped his hand. "Let's go back."

They flew, then fell. She landed in her body with a small jolt and a relieved gasp. Opening her eyes, she found Arthur kneeling beside the bed, worry wracking his features. How long had she been trapped in her nightmare on the astral?

"Thank you." She tried to reach out to touch his cheek, but the violent tremors in her hand disabused her of that notion. "Where's your mother? Is she all right?"

"I'm here." The chair creaked as Meg leaned forward, giving Morgan a clear view of just how the healing session had taken its toll on the other woman. Her eyes were sunken, her expression haggard, her usually impeccable hair in disarray. It was obvious that she had expended too much energy trying to heal Morgan and pull her back from the nightmare. Morgan knew she couldn't let her try again.

"I'm sorry," she whispered, the threat of tears stealing her voice. Clasping her hands together, she rested them against her forehead. She'd wait until she was alone to give in to the ramifications of her failure.

"You have nothing to apologize for, young lady," Meg admonished, her fatigue leaching some of the heat from her tone. "None of this is your fault."

Morgan looked away, not wanting to argue. Meg's exhausted state was very much her fault, as was Penny's death. As was the blight that had spread even further.

"Mrs. Davies." Dropping her hands, she sat up so that she could be in a less vulnerable position. "From the bottom of my heart, thank you for everything you've done. I'll-I'll return to the hotel for now and call my grandmother in the morning."

Arthur looked from her to his mother, a frown lowering his brows. He didn't like what her words meant, and neither did his mother. "We are not giving up," the older woman declared. "We just need to take the fight to the next level. I'll put out a call for other healers so we can form a healing circle. Three more would have us cover each cardinal direction, but five would include above and below. Thirteen would make a powerful circle. It will take a couple of days to bring everyone together and prepare for a cleansing ritual, but we can get it done, especially if it's at my cottage."

A couple of days. Morgan's hands twisted in her lap. She didn't know if she had that long, didn't know if she could endure another nightmare. Sensing her distress, Arthur tangled his fingers with hers. "I'll watch over you while you sleep in case you get attacked again. You can use this room, or I can guard you at the hotel."

She swung her legs over the side of the bed. "I can't let you do that."

"And I can't let you have another nightmare." He looked to his mother before looking back to her, his jaw a stubborn line. "That thing in your nightmare clawed at you, and the blight spread further. In your dream, not on the astral. If you have that dream again, it will attack you again. We can't let that happen."

She bit her bottom lip, considering. "How are you going to rest and watch me and do your work while your mother gathers other Light healers?"

"We can work something out. And there are other options. I have a colleague, she's an antiquities expert, and she's good at defusing cursed objects."

"This isn't a curse."

"I know that, but isn't a curse just a knot of Shadow? It's possible that she's come across something, heard something in the course of her work that could help us."

As much as she enjoyed his help and support, she had to stop it. "This isn't your fight, Arthur," she said, placing a hand on his knee as she kept her tone as gentle as she could make it. "You don't have to do this, especially for someone you just met."

A fierce fire lit his gaze as he wrapped his fingers around hers. "I know it's not my fight to fight. Still, I will stand beside you and fight as long as you do. It doesn't matter if I've known you for two days or two decades. I'll have your back. I'll be your sword and shield if need be. I won't…I won't stop trying until I've done anything and everything in my power to help you."

Her heart gave a funny little hop. The conviction of his declaration shot a bright bolt of hope through her, pushing Shadow back. He'd chased away the monster more than once. He could do so again while Meg got her circle together. Maybe this curse specialist woman could help. At least Morgan no longer felt alone in her fight.

She gave him a smile as she nudged him with her shoulder. "Who says chivalry is dead? Let's try everything we can, including your curse-fixing friend."

"Good." Arthur returned her smile, his thumb brushing circles on the back of her hand, making her insides flutter. "She's going to come 'round this evening to look at an antique ring I found for a client. We can talk to her then."

"Well." Meg slapped at her thighs before climbing to her feet, breaking the heady tension. "If my opinion means anything to you, Morgan, you should allow Arthur to help you. He's just proven his ability to bring you back. The bond you've already formed should help."

Morgan ducked her head. She guessed she and Arthur had been a teensy bit too obvious with their attraction for each other.

Meg turned to her son. "I know that I don't need to say this, but I expect you to protect Morgan if your friend tries to do something dangerous to remove the blight."

"I will."

"I'll call George to meet me over at the pub. You should stay here, Morgan, at least for tonight. Arthur's friend probably won't arrive until late evening."

"Okay." Morgan rose, holding tight to Arthur for support. "I think I'd like to go for a walk so I can clear my head. Maybe do some retail therapy at those holiday stalls at the castle. Then maybe we can grab something to eat and swing by my room so I can pick up a couple of things."

"Excellent idea," Meg said, giving Arthur a peculiar look. "That way you can be prepared for this evening."

Morgan had no idea what the other woman meant, but she had to figure curse-breaking was just as strenuous as Light healing, if not more. "May I give you a hug?"

Meg's expression softened. "Of course, you may."

Morgan wrapped her arms around the other woman, who returned the embrace with surprising strength. "Thank you, both of you, from the bottom of my heart. I don't know how I can ever repay you."

Meg stepped back, then cupped her cheeks, her eyes bright. "Just stay positive and focus on the Light. This is the season of miracles, after all."

Chapter Eight

"Can I help you with anything?"

"No, I'm just gathering a few necessary things." She scooped a collection of crystals from her nightstand, carefully nestling them inside a wooden box. "I should be ready in a couple of minutes."

Arthur consigned himself to the armchair below the window, watching as Morgan packed things into a carry-on-sized knapsack. The walk along the river to the castle's Folly and dinner in the Great Hall had done a world of good in improving Morgan's mood. The way she'd held his hand and rested her head on his shoulder had improved his.

Her ability to bounce back so completely amazed him. Would he be able to laugh at lame jokes as she had over dinner or hum offkey as he packed, as she was doing now? Or would he still be curled in a ball on the bed, cursing his fate, furious with the world?

He snorted. More likely he'd be down at the Boar and Knight, drinking his way through their supply of gin.

"Are you laughing at my ball gown?"

Her what? He caught a flash of red fabric spilling out of the closet. "You have a ball gown?"

"Yeah. For the Fire and Ice Ball that happens later in the week." She pulled it out so that he could see the ruby-red, strapless, and no doubt form-fitting gown that flared at the bottom. "My mother bought it and tickets for me in case your mother is able to heal me and give me a reason to celebrate."

"Your mother has exquisite taste. I'm sure it will look outstanding on you." Was she planning to attend alone?

She returned the gown to the closet, then closed the door with a decisive click. "Because things were going so well, I was going to ask you after today's session if you would be interested in going to the ball with me. And maybe staying for breakfast."

"Morgan." He shot to his feet. "You have to know the answer to both is yes."

"I know. If things were different, I think we might have already acted on this attraction and been well on our way to a wonderful holiday fling with literal magic sparks flying everywhere. This Shadowblight changed everything."

He stepped closer to her. "Everything?"

"Not everything," she answered with a rueful smile. "I'm attracted to you. Very attracted. That hasn't changed. If anything, it's grown."

She placed a hand on his chest, right over his wildly pounding heart. "How could I not be attracted to a handsome man with such a giving heart? A man who still has hope when it feels like all hope is lost?"

He reached up to cover her hand with his own. "How could I not be attracted to a woman who is beautiful inside and out? I've seen your spirit, seen its Light, seen how you've come back from things that would devastate lesser men and women. I have hope because I believe in you. I'm going to fight because you are worth it."

"Arthur." She leaned against him. "How's your shielding?"

"Fully set, as promised. Why?"

"Because I think we should kiss now."

"Shields at maximum. Fire away."

It would have been too easy to immediately lower his head and claim her lips, but he didn't want instant gratification. He wanted to savor the moment, savor her, sear this first kiss and everything about it so deep into his memory that his soul would feel it in the afterlife.

Cradling the back of her head, he brushed his lips against hers once, twice, three times. She made a small sound, a delicious promise that made him hungry for more. Dropping his free hand to her waist, he dragged her closer to claim his prize.

Stars. Morgan saw literal stars behind her eyelids, sparking a fire in her blood. She entwined her arms around Arthur's neck, wanting, needing to be closer. He groaned as she parted her lips, accepting her invitation to deepen the kiss.

They came up for air, resting their foreheads together, their breath harsh in the room's silence. "Morgan," he whispered, his tone aching and hungry and an echo of everything swirling inside her.

"I know." She leaned against him, trying to regain her equilibrium. "I know, but with what happened today—"

"That damned Shadowblight." He sighed and stepped back, reluctance in every motion.

She wrapped her arms around herself, missing his warmth. "Your mom fixed my shields, but this thing is sneaky. We can't take the chance that it won't jump to you while we're...distracted."

"Distracted." He chuffed out a laugh as he scrubbed a hand over his face. "You're the most beautiful distraction I've ever encountered, and I can't promise that I won't lose my shields and the rest of my senses during the heat of the moment. I appreciate you thinking about my well-being."

"Of course, I'm thinking about you," she retorted. "If anything happened to you because of me and the blight I carry, I think-I think that would break me."

He cupped her cheek. "You're not going to break, and I'm not going to get the blight. We're going to explore every option to rid you of the Shadowblight, and we're going to go to the ball together as planned. All good things are worth the wait, right?"

"Right." If their kiss was any indication, things were going to be very, very good. She was looking forward to that, forward to being free of the Shadow that had dogged her for so long.

He gave her a quick kiss then held her coat for her. "Let's get back to the flat."

After gathering everything she needed to stay overnight, they made their way out of the castle and back into town. Night had fully draped Caynham-on-Ledwyche in darkness, but the streets were still full of people coming and going from the various restaurants, dark silhouettes illuminated by the streetlamps and holiday lights. So she didn't think anything of the couple approaching them as Arthur unlocked the door leading to the apartment above the shop. Then a wall of power, Light and Shadow and something more, bumped against her senses. She shrank back, her flight response heartbeats away from kicking in. "Arthur?"

He turned as a woman pulled a dagger emanating a bright light. "Arthur," the woman said, her voice deathly quiet. "Step away. Something's not right with her."

"No." He threw out his arms, shielding her from the couple. "This is Morgan Lafayette. I told you about her. Morgan, this is Kira Solomon, the antiquities expert."

"Antiquities expert, my ass." Morgan's attempt at bravado fell flat, erased by fear. "She's a Shadowchaser."

The other woman sheathed her blade, obviously thinking Morgan wasn't enough of a threat to need her weapon. Then again, the silent man behind her was weapon enough. "And you are an American Light Adept with a huge Shadow problem. Which means you are now my problem."

"There's no need to scare her," Arthur admonished, then turned to Morgan. "Are you all right?"

"All right?" Hysterical laughter bubbled up. "She's a Shadowchaser come to kill me. Did you know that when you called her? Were you just tricking me all this time?"

She took a step back, hurt and betrayal pulling a hysterical laugh out of her chest. "All this time, I thought you wanted to help me. I thought you really were like the knight in shining armor version of you that I see on the astral. I-I thought our time together was something real."

Words scraped her throat raw as brimming tears watered down her vision. "None of it was real, was it? You were just placating me until the Shadowchaser got here."

"No, love, no." He captured her hands. "Kira really does remove curses from objects, and she truly is an expert in antiquities. I believe she can help you."

"Or she can kill me and move on to dessert." She looked at the Chaser. "That's what the other one did to my cousin. I wasn't even a teenager yet, but I remember. How do I know that you're actually here to help me? Why should I trust you?"

The Chaser laughed softly, a sound that made Morgan's hair stand on end. "I don't know who that Shadowchaser was, and I really don't care. I also don't care if you trust me or not, but we both trust Arthur. He asked me to help you. That's why you're still alive. If I didn't think you could be redeemed, we wouldn't still be standing here talking. Speaking of which, do you think you can set aside your prejudice long enough for us to see if I can help you? And while we're at it, maybe we could step inside so this drama doesn't play out in front of the locals?"

Arthur entwined his fingers with hers. "I already had an appointment with Kira to look at a cursed ring for me, as I'd mentioned earlier. I told her about the Shadowblight then asked for her help. Let's go inside and talk about it, all right?"

Morgan blinked, unable to believe that Arthur was on a first-name basis with a Shadowchaser. That he wasn't afraid of her. That he believed the Chaser not only could help but would.

What other choice did she have? If she tried to run, the Chaser or Mr. Silent-But-Deadly would be on her in a heartbeat. She didn't want to be put down like a stray on the street. Lafayettes weren't cowards.

"All right. If there's a chance, I want to take it."

With her resolve firmly fixed, she pulled up her big girl pants and summoned her Black Girl Magic attitude before she followed Arthur inside.

Chapter Nine

- -

Morgan returned from the toilet (thank goodness it wasn't as antique as the shop downstairs) to find Arthur and the Shadowchaser facing each other across his dining table. An intricate gold ring with a star ruby cabochon sat on a square of black velvet in front of Kira. She wore gloves, but not those white, lint-free gloves Morgan had seen archivists use when handling rare and precious objects, gloves like the ones Arthur currently wore. Kira's were cognac-colored leather instead, the soft, supple kind rich dudes used for driving their expensive sports cars. Morgan wondered why, but not enough to ask. No need to be rude to the person who held your life in their hands.

"Do you need more time?"

"No." Arthur rose, then gestured for her to take his seat as he carefully boxed up the ring. "It turns out that the ring has a minor curse, not a deadly one, and Kira gave me some clues to follow for its provenance. My client will be delighted."

Morgan sat, getting her first in-depth look at Kira. The Shadowchaser's appearance surprised her. She was young, maybe mid-twenties. At what age did the Gilead Commission recruit their Shadow-chasers? She should have been out partying with her girlfriends, not making life-and-death decisions. Her dark, coily hair was pulled back into a large pouf. She wore a white turtleneck beneath a black leather vest. Perfectly normal looking, if not for the facts that the silver collar necklace she wore looked sharp enough to behead someone, she kept her gloves on, and her eyes...well, Morgan didn't want to stare directly at her for too long. The Shadowchaser radiated power and danger in equal measure, making her wonder if she was fully human.

The silent man next to her, introduced as Khefar, was a mystery. Skin as dark as night, the sides of his head shaved with a cascade of black braids spilling over shoulders clad in a black leather jacket. Morgan could read nothing from him, Light or Shadow, just a large blank space with a hint of sun and sand. The blade he carried—how were they able to walk around with these weapons? —pulsed in a regular rhythm, as if it had a heartbeat. She didn't think there was anyone more dangerous than a Shadowchaser, but this man would be it, a coiled viper ready to strike.

"Morgan."

The Shadowchaser had an accent she couldn't identify, a mixture of places. "Yes?"

Kira folded her hands on the table. "Before I know whether I can help you or not, I need to know what I'm dealing with."

Morgan looked to Arthur, who'd taken the seat to her right, putting him across from the other man. "Arthur's mother said it was Shadow-blight."

"I'm sure she's right, but I need to see for myself."

"How are you going to do that?" Morgan wondered, hoping it didn't involve some sort of extrasense mind-meld with the Chaser.

"I'm going to touch you." The other woman pulled the glove free of her right hand. "Lay your left hand flat on the table, palm up."

"Kira."

Khefar hadn't moved, but with that one word, he became the most dangerous thing in the room. Morgan froze, her fight-or-flight instinct pegging hard to get-the-hell-out. If Shadowchasers were Gilead's nuclear option, what was this man who seemed ready to eviscerate anyone who glanced at Kira the wrong way?

Maybe it would have been touching and romantic if Morgan wasn't about to piss her pants.

Arthur splayed his hands on the table then stood, a glint of steel in his eyes and his tone as he glared at the other man. "I think it would be best if you back the fuck off and let Kira and Morgan handle this, don't you think?"

Damn. Morgan's terror vanished as her ovaries did a happy dance over Arthur's icy interjection. When all was said and done, she was totally and shamelessly going to throw herself at him.

"Khefar." Kira reached out to wrap her bare hand around Khefar's. The tension in the room evaporated as if it had never been. She then turned to face Morgan. "Don't worry, he's here to stop me if I go too far and harm you."

What the hell? Morgan turned to Arthur, who seemed just as perplexed. "Stop you from harming me?"

"I'm going to read you," the Shadowchaser said, giving an explanation but not an answer. "Just far enough back to see what happened to you."

That sounded simple enough, certainly not dangerous. "Okay."

"Twenty seconds," Kira said then, but Morgan wasn't sure if that was directed at her or Khefar. "That should be enough time. Morgan, your hand?"

Nervousness and a healthy dose of fear rose from Morgan's gut despite her attempts to hold it at bay. She had no idea what was about to happen, but it was dangerous enough to put the silent-but-deadly man on alert. She had to remind herself that the Shadowchaser could have easily taken her out when they'd first met. Morgan had no choice but to put faith in Arthur's assurance that Kira Solomon could help her.

With that in mind, Morgan laid her left hand on the table as instructed. The energy in the room shifted, coalescing around the Chaser in a bluish-white aura. "Do I need to drop my shields?"

A fleeting smile crossed Kira's lips. "Shielding doesn't matter if I have to touch you. We'll begin on three. One."

Kira pressed her index finger into the center of Morgan's palm. At first, she felt nothing, yet as soon as she opened her mouth to make a joke, she felt the Chaser's extrasense blow past her meager shielding and push into her palm. Fire danced along her nerve endings, through her veins, into her brain. Her vision grayed as her extrasense yielded to the devastating power of Kira's magic.

This must be what it's like to be buried by an avalanche, except it's an avalanche of electrical current. Fighting was futile even as the avalanche retreated, pulling Morgan's extrasense along with it. Flashes of memory escaped her mental grip, shreds of nightmares made all the more painful through Kira's magic. The gray of her vision darkened to black, and she welcomed it. Anything to escape the agony of having her extrasense ripped from her.

"That's enough!"

Morgan dimly heard the words but couldn't tell who had uttered them. She tried opening her eyes, but it took too much effort.

"Morgan!"

Arthur's tone, fraught with worry, broke through her pain-filled haze. She could see the bright white of his aura beside her, reaching for her. Drawn to him, she reached out mentally and physically, wanting to see him. His anxious expression swam in her vision. A sudden rush of vertigo had her sliding off the chair. Luckily Arthur caught her before she crashed to the floor.

"Are you all right?"

The urge to vomit crawled up her throat, accompanied by the urge not to embarrass herself further by ruining Arthur's shirt. A lie filled her throat but what came out was. "No. I don't think I am."

"I didn't use all the allotted time," Kira said as she pulled on her glove. "You should be fine in a few minutes."

Morgan swallowed hard. Not even twenty seconds, and she'd felt pain like that? "No wonder people are afraid of Shadowchasers."

Khefar folded his arms. "Kira is not like other Shadowchasers."

"It's okay," Kira said, her voice soft. She faced Morgan. "Are you afraid of me, Morgan?"

The loaded question put Morgan on the spot. There was no right way to answer, so she equivocated. "My family has good reason to be wary of Chasers."

"True." Kira dipped her head as if Morgan's non-answer was answer enough. "Arthur, do you have something stronger than tea? That should help her."

"Of course." He helped Morgan back into her chair before he disappeared. Being alone with the Chaser and her statue of a man bunched Morgan's shoulders. Could this be any more awkward? Not waiting for the other woman to bring up fear again, Morgan blurted out, "Did you see what you needed to see?"

"I did."

Something in Kira's tone and expression sent alarm flaring up Morgan's spine. Thank goodness Arthur returned, bearing four crystal cut tumblers and a matching decanter filled with amber liquid. She smiled at him as he pressed a generous portion into her hand and then poured three more servings. "Here."

Sure that no one was going to offer a toast, Morgan tilted the glass to her lips. Liquid fire seared her throat, a therapeutic burn that incinerated the remaining fog in her body and empowered her bravado. "What did you see, Kira?"

"Hhm." The Chaser adjusted her glasses. "What you faced while searching for the child was once a human who surrendered himself to Shadow. He was then consumed by Shadowblight. It's a parasite that's always voracious, always seeking a being to drain of its Light. The fucker."

A flash of yellow lit the Shadowchaser's eyes. "Shadowblight isn't something a Light Adept should have to face, no matter how powerful you and your family are. The Gilead field agents in charge of the region should have noticed the blight before you got involved, before that Shadow-consumed human took Penny. At the least, they should have sent a team to Savannah to support you. They didn't. They failed that child, they failed you, and they failed you again when you became infected, sitting on their collective asses while the blight eats away at you. All of this is not your fault."

A cough full of sobs escaped Morgann's throat. How long had she wanted to hear that from someone other than her family? Guilt released its death grip on her heart. Overcome, she tried to take another sip of the liquor, but her hands shook violently. Arthur wrapped his hands around hers, enabling her to take a fortifying swallow before returning the glass to the table. "Thank you for saying that."

"There's no reason to thank me."

Static electricity flooded the room. Kira's eyes flashed yellow behind her glasses as what could only be described as rage hardened her features. Morgan tensed, prepared to run until Khefar gripped Kira's chair, turned it around without a grunt, and leaned down. "Kira."

He said something in a language Morgan couldn't understand, but its impact was clear. Kira's fists loosened as she visibly wrestled her anger into submission. The static air subsided, and Morgan could once again breathe.

Kira cleared her throat, then turned back to Morgan. "I cannot officially speak for Gilead, but I will apologize on their behalf. I'm sure your father and your grandmother did what they could within the system, but the Gilead Commission is one giant bureaucracy. I will let Balm know what happened in Savannah and the lack of involvement from the field agents in the area. If they were afraid or unwilling to take it on, they should have contacted me. I need to find out why that didn't happen then inform Balm because such failure is unacceptable."

"I...uhm..." Morgan stuttered to a stop, her brain trying to make sense of everything that Kira had said. Was the Chaser really angry at Gilead's lack of action? A Shadowchaser siding with a Lafayette instead of against her? And what was that about informing Balm?

"Wait." She sat upright. "Are you saying there really is a Balm in Gilead? And Shadowchasers report directly to them?"

Humor crept into the other woman's gaze. "Yes, there really is a Balm, but Chasers answer to the Gilead Commission, of which Balm is the head. I answer to Balm."

The phrasing wasn't lost on Morgan. This Shadowchaser was different from the others. "Whoa."

"Let's just say that I have a special connection with Balm, so I can talk to her directly. And I will definitely talk to her about this."

This was surreal. Never had she thought she'd meet a Shadowchaser, and certainly not have tea with one. And certainly not a Shadowchaser who got angry on her behalf, criticized Gilead, and promised to talk to Balm, the embodiment of all things Light. Morgan didn't know much about Shadowchasers, but she had a feeling that Kira Solomon was different from the others. "Thank you, Kira."

"You're welcome." Kira clapped her hands together. "Okay, on to the most important thing right now. The Shadowblight."

Hope sprang like spring in Morgan's chest. "Does that mean you can cure me? You can remove the Shadowblight?"

***

Relief flooded Arthur as he squeezed Morgan's hand, her hope a palpable, incandescent glow that brightened the air around her. He'd done the right thing by asking for Kira's help. How fortuitous was it that Kira had arrived just in time?

He still gave Morgan a small burst of his extrasense, a move that had become habit every time they held hands. Even with Fate aligning as it had, they were dealing with Shadow. Nothing, not even Kira's help, was guaranteed. Their hope had to be tempered with reality.

Kira provided it. "Yes, I'm certain I can free you of the Shadowblight. Could I also kill you during the process of trying to save you? Possibly. I'm not going to tell you about the odds on that because I don't know them."

Morgan's crestfallen expression rankled him, but he managed to tamper his frustration well enough to ask, "Will you explain why it's so dangerous?"

Kira took a swallow of her Scotch before nodding. "In order to heal Morgan, I'll have to use my Lightblade to extract the blight. My blade's purpose is to eliminate Shadow. Does Meg have a sense of how far this blight has spread? Has it affected your bones or your nervous system? It could take minutes, hours, or longer to extract the Shadowblight from your system. I think it will be a painful process, and it may be more than you can take."

Rising, the Chaser pulled a beautiful but deadly blade from a sheath at her hip. It pulsed with an almost ultraviolet glow it hurt to see. Morgan gasped and shrank back, hiding behind Arthur's shoulder as Kira held the dagger aloft.

Kira nodded, acknowledging Morgan's action. "As you can see, my Lightblade senses when Shadow is nearby." She returned the dagger to its sheath and sat afterward. "Morgan, that fear you felt is the Shadowblight reacting to the power in my blade. When I attempt to extract it, there's a good chance that it will put up a fight. The more the Shadowblight fights, the more my Lightblade will fight. Your body will literally become a battlefield of Light versus Shadow."

A fist of ice clenched Arthur's guts. He turned to Morgan, wrapping an arm about her shoulders as she shuddered. "There's got to be something we can do to lessen the pain for her."

"I believe so." Kira looked at him and Morgan. While he knew the Shadowchaser was harsh to a fault, she wouldn't offer hope if there was none to be had. "Can your mother gather a coven of Light healers and Adepts by day after tomorrow?"

"In two days?" While he desperately wanted Morgan to be healed as soon as possible, he didn't think his mother could gather a dozen Light Adepts and healers on such short notice. "That's Yule."

"And the Winter Solstice," Kira reminded him. "Yes, it's the longest night, and Shadow will be strong, but since it also celebrates the return of the sun, a circle of Light should be enough to deal with it while I heal Morgan."

That was all he needed to hear. He quickly pulled out his phone to ring his mother. "Mum, I've got you on speaker. Morgan is with me and so is Kira Solomon and her partner, Khefar."

"Light and blessings to you, Shadowchaser Solomon, and to you, Khefar."

Arthur blinked. He'd never heard his mother use such a formal tone before, nor in Kira's response. "Light and blessings to you, Healer Davies. I need a favor."

"If it's in my power to do, I'll do it."

"We've been discussing Morgan's Shadowblight problem," Kira said. "I believe there's a way to remove it."

"Thank the Light." Arthur heard his mother's heavy sigh of relief clearly through the speaker. "What can I do to assist?"

"I'm hoping you can gather enough Light healers and Adepts to cast a circle," Kira told her. "Do you think that's possible?"

"When?"

"Two nights from now."

"That's Winter Solstice." His mother's tone was thoughtful. "I've already reached out to a few solitary practitioners, but I'm not sure I can get more than a half-dozen. I'll send out a call in our private chat group, hopefully we'll get others in."

"I might be able to get more," Morgan chimed in.

Arthur turned to her. "You can?"

"We're talking about eliminating the Shadowblight inside me. I'm not just going to sit on my ass while the rest of you do all the work." She pulled out her own phone to make a call, which was answered immediately.

"How are things going over there?"

"We're well," Morgan answered. "Ma Belle, I'm here with Arthur, Meg's son. She's on speakerphone. Kira Solomon is also here, and she's the Sha—"

"I'm aware of her identity," the voice said, sounding too young and strong to be a grandmother. "Light and blessings to you, Chaser Solomon."

"Light and blessings to you, Matriarch Lafayette."

Again, the formal exchange of words. Yet something in Kira's tone signaled something more...respectful? Cautious? Morgan's family, in general, and grandmother, in particular, had to be far more than she'd told him.

"My granddaughter sounds astonishingly well for having met a Shadowchaser," the matriarch mused. "May I take hope from that?"

"Ma Belle," Morgan said. "Kira believes there's a way she can remove the Shadowblight, but she needs a circle of Light Adepts and healers for Solstice. Ms. Meg might be able to get around six, so I was wondering if you could get some Lafayette members at Adept level to Caynham-on-Ledwyche the day after tomorrow."

"If?" The Lafayette matriarch's laughter rang through the room. "If?"

Morgan snorted. "I didn't want to presume."

"Your parents and I will be there," Morgan's grandmother said, her tone brisk. "Bethany will come, too. It's just a matter of deciding who else is close enough and strong enough to get the privilege. I'll limit the amount of people by how many a charter jet can hold. We'll be there sometime tomorrow."

"Thank you, Ma Belle." Morgan choked out. "Thank you."

"As if we'd leave you alone during this time. Not that you're alone. Arthur?"

A jolt of surprise stiffened his spine. "Yes, ma'am?"

"Thank you for taking care of our Morgan," the matriarch said. "Her parents and I look forward to meeting you tomorrow, and I'll be glad to see your mother again. Meg, shall we all have lunch together?"

"Of course," his mother said, pleasure and amusement threading her tone. "My home is open to you and yours. I'll make something special for the six of us."

Suddenly, the call sounded less like a request for Light healers and Adepts and more like a meeting of families for a couple. And how did the matriarch know that he had been taking care of Morgan? What did her grandmother mean by "taking care" of her? Did she somehow know how he felt about Morgan?

Morgan gave his hand a hard squeeze. He immediately locked down his shields, afraid he'd been broadcasting. She held her phone up. "Thank you, Ma Belle. There's a big ol' hug waiting for you when you get here."

She disconnected. Arthur prepared to say goodbye to his mother, but Kira raised her hand. "Healer Davies, is there a place we can cast a circle in private? We'll probably need the full night, sunset to sunrise, and as much earth magic as we can pull."

"We can cast the circle behind my house," his mother answered. "It's relatively private and connects to a field that leads to Mortimer Forest, which has standing stones in it. Their power flows toward my cottage, and I often tap into it."

"Perfect." Kira slapped her hands together. "We'll need all the power we can get."

Arthur frowned as he ended the call with his mother. Something seemed off with Kira's words, as if he'd missed a critical point. Looking at the hope and happiness brimming in Morgan's eyes, however, he was loath to dampen the upbeat mood.

He gathered her hands in his. "It's going to be fine. Kira and the healers will strip the Shadowblight away. Two days from now, you'll be free, and after Yule, we'll go to the ball to celebrate."

"I can't tell you how much I'm looking forward to being free of this burden." Doubt tempered her smile. "But something's off."

Damn. Had he broadcasted his doubts to her? Before he could allay her concern, she turned to Kira.

"Earlier, you said you'd just use your Lightblade to get rid of the Shadowblight, so why do you need a circle of healers *and* Adepts?"

Kira gazed at them, her eyes serious behind her tinted lenses, as if she was considering how to say what needed to be said. Beside him, Morgan nodded. "I know you won't lie, so your hesitation must mean the reason is either very bad for me or very serious for all of us."

"Yes." The Chaser folded her arms on the table then leaned forward. "I'm pretty sure that I can remove the Shadowblight with the help of a few healers if necessary. Unfortunately, that may not be enough. It could return."

"Of course." Morgan lowered her head. "Everything was falling into place so easily it was hard to believe. I don't—I don't think I can handle it if I wake up one day and the Shadowblight is back. I—we—can't let that happen!"

Arthur hauled Morgan into his lap, wrapping her in his arms as tightly as he could without hurting her. It probably wasn't his right to do so, not yet anyway, but he didn't care, just as he didn't care about Kira and her silent guardian looking on. "Kira said *could*, love," he told her, stroking her hair. "There's no guarantee that it will come back."

"There's no guarantee that it won't, either." She straightened, wiping beneath her eyes carefully before blowing out a breath. "Unless there *is* a surefire way to keep it gone for good. Is there?"

"There has to be," Arthur assured her. "Otherwise, Kira wouldn't have requested Light Adepts as well as healers. Isn't that right?"

Kira nodded. "Morgan, when I touched you, I saw how you were infected. Only a portion of that Shadowling's blight got inside you. I can seal it for a time so that it doesn't spread more, but it could awaken at any time. The only way to make sure the blight doesn't hurt you more is to kill the source."

"But the source is on the astral plane," Arthur pointed out.

"I know. That's why we need the circle." The Chaser glanced between them. "Khefar and I need you two to transport us to the astral plane. We'll lure the original Shadowling to us then destroy it. Once we return, the healers and I will remove the weakened Shadowblight from Morgan's body."

"Lure it?" Arthur asked. "Do you really think that thing will come to us, knowing that one of us is a Shadowchaser?"

It was Morgan who answered. "It will come if we use me as bait."

Chapter Ten

- -

"**A**bsolutely not!"

Morgan jumped at the vehemence in Arthur's words. She slid back into her seat as he stood, ears reddening. "There is absolutely no way we're going to use Morgan as bait to destroy that thing. She shouldn't travel on the astral at all!"

Morgan's eyebrow lifted of its own accord. Even her parents had given up announcing absolutes over her once she'd reached adulthood. As scared as she was, as much as a tiny voice cheered on his objections, she couldn't let them slide without saying something. She stood, ready to educate him on agency and her right to decide, but Kira intervened.

The Chaser folded her arms, expression cold as she looked at Arthur. "That's not your call to make."

"Just as it's not what I asked you to do when I requested your help," Arthur shot back, his features fiery red with anger. "I wanted you to heal her, not turn her into a sacrifice!"

He threw a gesture at Khefar. "How would you like it if someone wanted to turn your woman into a sacrifice?"

Khefar retained his stony expression, his words dropping like shards from a glacier. "There is no retirement home for Shadowchasers. Kira sacrifices herself almost daily to stand against Shadow. It is her calling and her duty."

Morgan's mouth dropped as she watched the man walk towards Kira before taking her hand. "And it is my honor, my privilege, and my great fortune to be able to stand and fight beside her so that she can live as well as she can for as long as she can."

Wow. Morgan didn't know about Kira, but she was touched and humbled by Khefar's words, words she was sure he didn't say often. Based on Kira's expression, she was right.

Kira turned into his shoulder for a moment, her back to the room. "If you keep this up, you're going to make me lose my badass reputation. Stop it." She punched his shoulder for emphasis.

The warrior—really, he couldn't be anything but—smiled. A real, authentic smile that clearly was for Kira alone. Morgan turned away, wanting to let them have their moment. She pressed a fist to her heart as a flash of jealousy flared inside her. That was the kind of relationship you wanted when you had no choice but to fight, no matter the odds.

Her gaze tangled with Arthur's. Her thoughts must have clearly shown on her face because his red anger receded, replaced by care and concern. He sighed as he gripped her shoulders. "Please reconsider. That's all I ask. This is dangerous. The thought of using you like this terrifies me."

"Imagine how it feels from where I'm standing." She understood his fear. Panic drenched her bloodstream, urging her to give in to Arthur's demand and run as fast and as far as she could. That was the Shadowblight talking, and she'd be damned if she'd allow some Shadow parasite to control her. She knew she couldn't give in. Arthur knew it too, but she still had to say it out loud for everyone.

She reached up to cover his hands with her own, feeling his extrasense, his power, his care. "Arthur, you said it yourself. That thing you saw in my nightmare is the same dragon-like thing you've been guarding against. You may have thought you were protecting your town, but what if it's been after you all this time, since you're a traveler like me?"

Painful realization darkened his eyes. She tightened her grip on his hands. "Yes, I'm scared. Yes, I know I could die on the astral plane if that thing gets a chance to finish what it started. But I'm also scared that it could get to you somehow. I can't stay here and do nothing. That's certain death. Even if Kira successfully kills the Shadowblight inside me, one day, she or another Shadowchaser is going to have to create a final solution if the blight returns. I have better odds of surviving if we take the fight to the astral and kill that thing there. With Kira and Khefar fighting with us, I have absolute confidence that we'll win, and I'll be healed. I need you to believe that, too."

She gave him what she hoped was a smile and not a grimace as she cupped his cheek. "Besides, it's my body carrying the blight. Shouldn't it be my choice to determine how I contribute?"

"I know. I know it here." He touched his forehead, followed by his chest. "But in here, I want to wrap you in a thousand layers of bubble cushion wrap and hide you in a tower of Light that no one else can enter."

"Arthur." Her heart tripped over itself. Overcome, she wrapped her arms around his waist and pressed her face against his thudding heart. There was no longer any doubt about her feelings for this man, who would take on anyone, even a Shadowchaser, to keep her safe. "I'm grateful that I have you in my corner. But I need you to understand, I need to be the hero in my own story. I can't just sit on my ass while everyone else is risking their lives for me. That wouldn't be fair to them or to me."

"But we don't know if we can bring someone to the astral with us. What if we try, and it's just us facing that thing?"

She pulled back to see him. "Then you'll defend me like you did before, and we'll come back just as we did before and figure out another way."

He released a heavy sigh, his lips twisting as if to prevent more words from escaping. She could clearly see the struggle in those gorgeous eyes, then the anguish, and finally acceptance. "How can I stand to lose you when I've just found you?"

"Then don't lose me." She gave him a wink to lighten the mood and keep her own tears at bay. "I don't want to lose you either. Our date for the Frost and Flame ball will be my first official one in almost two years. I have no plans to miss it, okay?"

"Okay." Finally, he released a smile before turning to Kira. "We need to make a plan."

"The plan is pretty simple." Kira held up a hand, ticking each action item off. "First, all of us make it to the astral. Second, Morgan drops her shielding and calls the Shadowling in. Third, Arthur and I take point on attacking the creature with Morgan as backup and Khefar as the last resort. Fourth, we— "

"Excuse me." Arthur held up a hand, and Morgan was sure he intended to ask the question that also came to her mind. "Why is Khefar the last resort?"

"Do not misunderstand, Arthur Davies," the other man said. "I will defend, I will fight, but I will not draw this blade unless all hope is lost."

Morgan frowned. Did that make even a bit of sense? "Won't it be too late then?"

A mask devoid of everything dropped over Kira's features. "If Khefar draws his blade, you both need to drop back to this plane immediately."

"And leave you two behind?" Arthur questioned, his eyebrows to his hairline. "There had better be a compelling reason for that."

A scary smile bowed the Shadowchaser's lips. "If you think Shadowchasers are the nuclear option, consider Khefar and the Dagger of Kheferatum a supernova."

With a name like that, Morgan couldn't help but think the blade was dangerous, more dangerous than the warrior and the Chaser facing them. "The dagger. Is it that bad?"

Kira looked to Khefar, as if asking permission. When he nodded, she continued. "What I'm about to say stays in this flat. Understood?"

"Of course," Morgan and Arthur said in unison.

"The Dagger of Kheferatum is a godsblade."

"Godsblade?"

Kira nodded. "I don't know how much you know about Egyptian mythology, but Atum is the first and last god. Creator and destroyer. The dagger was forged from Atum."

"The dagger is a part of Atum," Khefar added. "Made from a metal not of this world, part of the primordial mound, and part of his power and flesh. That means it can create, but its main desire is to unmake things."

"So unmaking the Shadowblight would be a good thing, right?" Morgan wondered. "You can unmake the Shadowling, then unmake the blight inside me."

Khefar slapped his hand over the hilt of the blade at his hip to keep it from unsheathing. No, she had to be imagining things. There's no way she saw the dagger move on its own before Khefar could stop it.

"Do not suggest such things," he cautioned. "There is no need to wield a dagger when a scalpel is needed."

"Exactly." Kira nodded for emphasis. "If he unsheathes that dagger on the astral plane, it could do what Khefar wants it to do, or it could decide to unmake that plane entirely, and us along with it."

Silence. Morgan watched Arthur struggle for words before speaking. "Okay then. Khefar and his dagger are the 'we're about to die anyway' plan. I'd rather not get to that point, so what other options are there?"

"Kira." A flash of insight struck Morgan. "It's still early on the other side of the ocean. Maybe we should call my grandmother. When I was attacked and trapped, my father found me and brought me back. It's a good possibility he knows how to take a non-traveler to the astral plane and the best way to fight. He's been a traveler longer than I've been alive. He might even be able to take both you and Khefar without our help. Problem is, it's almost a sure bet that he'll also object to me going to the astral."

"Then how do we solve that problem?" Khefar asked.

"That's why I want Kira to call my grandmother," Morgan answered. "My dad is my dad, but Ma Belle is the matriarch. No one in the Lafayette clan would dare go against her."

"That is now plan A," Kira decided. "I'll temporarily seal the Shadowblight then call Belle Lafayette to coordinate everything we need. After that's done, everyone needs to spend time resting and recharging, gathering as much Light as possible."

"Okay." Morgan unlocked her phone and handed it to Arthur. "Why don't you call my grandmother and let her know what the plan is?"

"Me?" His eyes widened. "You want me to call your grandmother and have our first conversation be about this very dangerous plan? That's not the first impression I want to make."

She squeezed his bicep. "I have a feeling that my grandmother chatted with your mother as soon as we disconnected. She's probably waiting to hear from you."

"I..." He looked at her, then down to the phone, then back to her. "I, uhm. God, I need to prepare for this."

Chapter Eleven

Nerves wound tight beneath Morgan's skin as she placed the towel Kira had requested over the back of the chair they'd brought to Arthur's room with them. She tried to tell herself that the nerves were about being in Arthur's bedroom for the first time and not about the Shadowchaser waiting for Morgan to remove her sweater and bra.

"The Shadowblight is only on your back, right?" Kira asked.

Morgan nodded as she straddled the chair with her chest pressed against its back, then unhooked her bra. "From the picture that Ms. Meg showed me, yes."

"Then all you need to do is expose your back," Kira said then. "I just need the blight fully uncovered."

"Uhm, before you start, I have a question."

"Go on."

"Wouldn't it be a waste of your energy to seal the blight now since we're going to face it on the astral a couple of days from now?"

Kira tilted her head. "You mean that you don't want those blight-free nights with Arthur?"

"Ah. Uhm, well." Heat stamped her cheeks. "Picked up on that, huh?"

"Knowing how to read the room is a necessary part of my job," the Chaser answered with a slight bow to her lips. "It doesn't take extrasense to realize that something is simmering between you two."

"Is it that obvious?"

"How could I not know?" Kira snorted. "Arthur's not subtle on the best of days. Like I could miss it when he pulled you into his lap. Then there was the whole 'how can I lose you when I've just found you' thing. Besides, you were a little touchy-feely yourself."

Embarrassment burned through Morgan hotter than being half-naked in front of the Chaser. "We really won't have anything to worry about?"

"You won't have to worry about the Shadowblight being an obstacle between you two," Kira corrected. "And as long as you don't attempt to travel to the astral plane, the blight will remain sealed."

"Oh, good." She slumped in relief. Despite everything that had happened since she'd met Kira, Morgan still wanted to be with Arthur. Because of everything that had happened since she'd met Kira, she knew that she and Arthur had to make the most of the next two days. The day after Yule wasn't a guarantee for any of them but especially not for her.

"For what it's worth, Arthur sounded genuinely happy to meet a fellow traveler, and I quote, 'a lovely one at that.' That says something, don't you think?"

"I hope so." Morgan forced herself not to hunch her shoulders, not knowing how close the blade's tip was to her skin. "I'm drawn to him in a way I haven't been drawn to anyone."

"Hhm." That one sound held a wealth of thought. Morgan gritted her teeth and waited tensely until Kira spoke again. "It almost feels as if a greater work is happening. There are hundreds of Light healers in the Americas, many I'm sure the Lafayette matriarch knows personally. So why did she send you to Arthur's mother? Were you meant to meet him all along? And it just so happens to be when Khefar and I are supposed to meet with him. Maybe we're intended to gather here to destroy the Shadowblight."

"If that's true, that's the best news I've heard since I was inflicted with this. Encounters with the Shadowblight had to have happened before. If we can destroy it, I can die happy."

"I prefer we all survive happy," came Kira's retort.

"Duly noted." Trying to keep her tone as blithe as possible, Morgan drew in a breath and gripped the chair spindles. "Let's do this."

"Now you're eager." Kira snorted. "I know it seems impossible but try to relax. My Lightblade won't pierce your skin, but I do need to trace a Light barrier around the blight as close as possible."

"Is this going to hurt?"

"Probably," came Kira's blunt reply. "You are roughly twenty percent Shadowblight, which means it's strong enough to put up some resistance when I begin to seal it. I don't know what that could do to you."

"That explains why you demanded that I step away from Arthur when we first met," Morgan tried to joke, feeling a little light-headed. She was twenty percent Shadowblight? How much longer did she have until fifty percent? Would she still be considered herself then? No. Kira would probably eliminate her first. "The blight must have recognized you as a threat. I suppose I should thank you for not killing me first and asking questions after."

"That's not my way, especially when it comes to humans," Kira said. "Even then, between Light and Shadow is the gray of Balance. I find that most beings are trying to live their lives the best they can. There are some born of Shadow who walk toward the Light, and there are some born of Light who fall into Shadow. Then there are those who are neither and those who are both."

Morgan felt a blush of heat on her right shoulder as Kira began her work. The tip of Kira's blade slid along Morgan's skin like hundreds of tattoo needles outlining the blight in micrometers. If this was the worst that the pain would get, she'd deal with it, but she needed their conversation to distract her. "How is it possible to be both? Does that mean I can be both?"

"It's possible because of the gray, the fulcrum called Balance between Light and Shadow." Kira snorted. "I sound like I know what the hell I'm talking about, don't I? As close as I am to Balm, she's not going to tell me what she doesn't want me to know, and even then, she'd prefer that I learn it on my own. I guess mothers are like that."

A gargled cough-gasp stuck in Morgan's throat like an oversized wad of gum. "Did you just imply that Balm, as in the Balm of Gilead, the head of all things Light, is your mother?" she asked, pain a distant memory.

"Adopted mother," the Chaser clarified. "From what I understand, she and my birth mother were close."

A thousand questions she didn't dare utter bounced on Morgan's tongue like hail on pavement. She settled on what she considered the safest one. "Are all Shadowchasers like you?"

"No idea." Kira's gloved hand touched her shoulder, and heat blossomed beneath Morgan's skin. "It's not like Chaser Con is a thing. I've only met one other Shadowchaser, but I don't know where he is now."

Beneath the circumspect tone lurked something...sad? Tired? Being a Shadowchaser had to be a solitary job with very few people, if any, happy to see them. "It must help a lot to have Khefar with you."

"It does." The heat in Morgan's shoulder faded as Kira paused her work. "He's already kept me from dying once, and I returned the favor. I don't take that for granted though. In the end, it's me who decides whether I stand or fall. Luckily, he also keeps me in check."

Morgan wasn't sure what that meant but decided she didn't need to know. She had the feeling that she'd already learned more about the Shadowchaser than any non-Gilead member had. "Are you telling me all of this so I won't focus on the pain or because you know I'm taking this info to my grave in two days?"

Despite the glove, Kira's fingers dug into Morgan's shoulder hard enough to hurt. "I'm not spending my time sealing you just so you can die two days from now. I don't waste my energy like that."

Morgan hunched her shoulders in a poor effort to dodge the verbal blow. "I'm sorry. My emotions are all over the place right now."

"Some of those emotions are directed toward Arthur. Do you want him to come in and help you? The pain will probably intensify from here."

Heat swept out of Morgan's heart, flooding over the pain between her shoulder blades to engulf her throat, her cheeks, and her chest. "You've known him longer than I have. Is it a good idea for a man who's literally a knight in shining armor on the astral plane to come in here to help?"

Kira chuffed out a laugh. "I see you know his behavior very well."

"Only a bit." What she didn't know should have bothered her. In normal circumstances, maybe it would have been a warning sign. But what she did know about him—his extrasense, his traveling ability, his desire to save—called to her on an almost molecular level, as if he was a missing part of her. As if, now that she'd met him, she'd be incomplete without him. "You seem to know him pretty well since he has your phone number and all."

"I've known him for a few years. I met him through my late mentor, who worked at the British Museum. Arthur has a habit of finding magical artifacts. He'd come across some antiquities of unknown provenance, and Bernie called me to assist."

Surprise temporarily blocked the agony spiraling up from Morgan's shoulder blade. "What?"

"Surprise. I'm not just a Shadowchaser. Arthur only knew that I could use my extrasense to read objects, dissolve virulent curses, and uncover provenance. We worked together on other antiquities, but he didn't discover that I'm a Shadowchaser until his wife was killed by a Shadowling that had escaped a binding casket. He'd tried to save her but couldn't. I promised him that I would hunt down and kill the Shadowling that had attacked her. And I did."

"Oh." Morgan's heart clenched. She remembered her talk with Arthur on the astral when they'd commiserated in shared grief over failing to save lives. His grief had made it clear that it had been someone dear to him, but she'd assumed his father, not a wife. She didn't know how long ago it was, but it didn't matter. Grief, guilt, and anger had their own schedules.

Tears pooled beneath her lashes, but Morgan wasn't sure if they were from pain or sadness or both. "He must have suffered so much."

"He did. It was almost four years ago, and he just now seems like his old self. That must be because of you. How long have you and Arthur been together?"

"I—ow!" Pain splashed like seawater across her face, leaving behind burning, salty tears. "A few days ago, but when our magics met, it felt like a reunion of sorts. There were literal sparks and a connection, but…"

"What?"

"His behavior toward me. Do you think it's only because he feels compelled to save me to compensate, or do you think it's something else?"

"You two are the only ones who can answer that. I don't know much about the something else stuff. The guy I'm seeing is 4500 years older than me, and I'm pretty sure he's still fudging his true age. He's got his reasons to stay beside me, and we're enjoying each other's company while we can. Carpe diem."

4500…she meant Khefar? Morgan's brain refused to compute, focusing on pain instead. "Enjoy each other's company while we can. I think that sums it up."

She hunched her shoulders against another needlelike stab of pain. "It's really burning now, like my back is about to crack open with lava."

"I'm about forty percent done. Can you hold out?"

Not even halfway done? Morgan forced words past the lump in her throat. "Can you pause long enough for me to get to the bed? I think I should lie down now."

"Okay." Morgan gasped as something snatched at her spine. "Move carefully."

She easily obeyed the order simply because the room spun enough at that slow walk. Kira shifted her blade to her left hand to shake out her right, and that's when Morgan noticed that the Lightblade's shape had changed to something more like a scalpel. Lightblades could change shape? Probably made it easier to travel with the blade if it could change from a dagger to a fountain pen or something.

Struggling to remain upright, she shakily shucked her shoes then stretched out on the bed as Kira dragged the chair closer. "Just focus on the fact that with the Shadowblight sealed, you won't have to worry about being shielded with Arthur."

"Kira?"

The excruciating agony dropped from 1000 to 999 as the Chaser paused her work. "Yes?"

"I'm close to passing out, but I just want you to know that I'm okay with the hope-it-doesn't-come-to-this plan."

"Hhm." The burning began again. "What do you think that plan is?"

"Have the blight take me over completely, and just before I lose my humanity, you take your Lightblade and kill me."

Silence, save for the blood pounding like war drums between Morgan's ears. Finally, the Shadowchaser spoke. "I don't want it to come to that."

"I don't either," Morgan gasped, a frail laugh seeping out of her. "But I know we can't leave that thing out there. There can't be another Penny. There can't be another me."

"Arthur and your family won't like that."

"I know." Morgan sniffled, wiping her face on the towel bunched in her fist. "They may even hate you for it."

"It wouldn't be the first time or the last."

"I-I'm sorry!" She bit down on her lips to keep from screaming as the blight wriggled and writhed as if trying to break free. Flames seared their way up and down her spinal cord in waves of increasing agony.

"Morgan, let go. Enough of the blight is contained that you don't have to be conscious to help me. You can let—"

Another burst of pain fulminated like a nuclear cloud, stealing her breath and her consciousness.

Chapter Twelve

"How are you feeling?"

Morgan laughed as she squeezed her hair with a towel one final time. "Even better than the last three times you asked me since I woke up. A short nap and a long shower have me almost feeling like myself again."

"A short nap?" he echoed. "You were unconscious, not asleep."

"Okay, a short period of unconsciousness, then sleeping." She smirked at him. "I distinctly remember dreaming about you sitting there watching me like a hawk, or maybe a vulture. Sorta like what you're doing now."

He watched as she dug into her overnight bag for some sort of cream that she then worked into her auburn-brown coils. He couldn't tell her how long he'd sat beside her, holding her hand, wrapping her in his extrasense, willing her to wake, fearing that she wouldn't. Hearing her light snore, feeling her fingers flexing against his, then staggering through the almost unbearable relief that had nearly crushed him the moment she'd opened her eyes and smiled at him.

Now she stood before him, soft and warm from her shower, her hair in damp coils, her face free of makeup, and her body draped in a two-piece pajama set that displayed a distractingly large amount of skin despite the silky robe that draped her shoulders. "What else should I be looking at when you're the most beautiful thing in my flat?"

"The things you say and the way you say them...I'm defenseless." She turned from the mirror to face him in that moment, her smile its own reward. Concern quickly replaced it. "Have you heard from Kira? How is she? Where are they staying if the hotels and inns are full?"

"I rang them while you showered. I'm sure Gilead has a safe place not too far away. Khefar said she's worn out, but she's had food and rest. Which you need as well."

She secured her hair with one of those stretchy things, looking at him with hooded eyes. "Thanks to that unconscious napping I did, I'm refreshed now. As for food, we had a decent meal before I packed a bag and came home with you. So, we ate, we drank, and we worked out a plot to save the world. Now it's time to be merry, remember?"

"I remember." That seemed like something that had happened days ago, not a few hours earlier. The flirtatious brushes of their extrasense, the sensual promise percolating between them, before it had all gone to hell and terror had set in. "I also remember what happened after, what happened while I waited for you to regain consciousness."

"Ah." A world of weight in that one word. "You saw it."

Concern shot through him anew at the sudden change in her demeanor. "What happened? What do you mean, saw it? Saw what?"

"The Shadowblight on my back. You saw it, didn't you?"

"You showed me on the astral," he reminded her. Was that accusation in her tone? "As for here, you were covered and unconscious when I came in after Kira was done, and I'm not the kind of man who'd ogle an unconscious woman. So no, I don't know what the mark looks like."

"I'll show you." She slipped the robe from her shoulders, allowing the silky fabric to slide to the floor. "You need to get a good look at it before...anyway, I should show it to you."

Part of him wanted to dissuade her, but the other part of him, the concerned and curious part, wanted to urge her on. Yet the seriousness in her tone, the solemn look she gave him, rendered him mute.

Next, she slipped the straps of the top down her arms and off one at a time, until the material barely covered the rise of her breasts. He made a valiant effort to look into her eyes, but his other senses demanded his focus. The desire to draw her close, to touch her, to taste her, hear her moans as he kissed her and reveled in her honey-vanilla scent prodded him to suit action to thought.

Then she turned around, and he couldn't swallow down his shocked gasp.

Her entire back, from the nape of her neck to the rise of her buttocks, was covered with what at first seemed like henna artwork, as if someone had taken black body paint and sketched a garden onto her back. Vines and flowers swirled across her skin as if on a trellis. Except this wasn't paint. This wasn't art. This was Shadowblight, and it had spread far more than he'd imagined.

"Kira said that I'm about twenty percent Shadow," Morgan spoke into the charged silence, her voice remote, her posture stiff as if doing so helped her contain her emotion. "It grew some when I had that setback with your mother, but I didn't realize how much until Kira snapped a pic on her phone and showed it to me."

Hollow laughter pushed past her lips. "No wonder she drew her Lightblade the moment she saw me."

"Morgan…" A protective surge overrode shock. He attempted to reach out with his extrasense, but he couldn't feel her. It was as if she'd turned her shielding into a castle wall, thick and impenetrable.

"I didn't know it was this bad." Her voice flattened to nothing. "The reason it took so long to seal it is because Kira had to trace around the blight, carving a Light barrier around each part so that it wouldn't spread more. It felt like getting a tattoo the old-fashioned way. She did it so that we—so that I—could have a couple of days without having to worry about the blight spreading more than it has."

She turned, slipping her top back into place, her gaze bouncing everywhere but to him. "I trust Kira. If she says we're safe, I believe her, but just because the blight is sealed doesn't mean there's no risk to you. Especially since your extrasense, the Light inside you, is so bright and attractive…"

She straightened her shoulders, her gaze now clear and direct on him. "If this changes things between us, I understand. The last thing I want to do is risk exposing you to the blight. Even with a Shadowchaser's seal, things could go sideways, so if you want us to rethink this, it's okay."

The smile she gave him was too tight, too bright, the stance of her body too rigid. She didn't have to say it to know that she expected him to reject her. Words crawled up his throat, trapped and unspoken, despite his attempts to free them.

"No harm, no foul," she told him, her voice and tone brittle as she waved her hands. "I've asked you for too much already. We can pretend we never made those types of plans, and I'll crash on your couch tonight. Better yet, I can just go back to the hotel and then meet up with you and your mother when my family arrives. I'll go get dressed."

She wanted to leave? Just the idea of Morgan walking away from him was too much. Being with her, being intimate with her wasn't the danger. The true danger was in letting her walk away. If he let her leave like this, it would be the end of everything, and nothing was more important than that.

Her head lowered as she attempted to butt past him. His muscles unlocked, his hand shooting out to grab her wrist, to spin her around. The moment she crashed against him was the moment his lips crashed against hers. She resisted, and for a terrifying moment, he believed that he'd acted too late, that he'd have to let her go. Then a tremor swept her, and the hands that had pushed at his chest now gripped at his shoulders as she sighed against his mouth.

"I'm not letting you go," he growled against her lips. "Don't even think it."

"Aren't you afraid of me now?" she asked, her voice thick.

"No. Never."

He wasn't afraid of her. He was afraid of what they had yet to face. Afraid that he wouldn't be able to stand beside her, to fight with her. Afraid of all the things that could go wrong, afraid of the what-ifs that threatened to choke him. But afraid of her? Never.

No more words or dark thoughts, only action. He claimed her mouth again, wanting to kiss away her doubts, their fears. After every painful moment she had endured under Kira's Lightblade, and she thought he'd abandon her?

With a low whimper, she threw her arms around his neck, plastering her scantily clad body against his. His extrasense burned like lava through his senses, demanding more. Everything she'd endured, everything she had gone through, spurred him on. He would pleasure her until they could think of nothing else. He'd give her as much pleasure as she could handle, and then he'd give her more. Make her forget everything except him. Make her forget the past and the future to focus solely on the now.

Still kissing her, he palmed her buttocks to lift her up, giving a grunt of satisfaction when she wrapped her legs about his waist. His knees nearly buckled as he felt the heat of her core low on his belly, close, but not close enough. Desire blazed into hunger, his hindbrain demanding that he claim her.

She cupped his cheeks, her tongue teasing his as he bumped into every wall and opening between the bathroom and the bedroom. He tightened his grip on her, wanting to get inside her, needing to get inside her, as if she could be shelter when desire was the storm that raged inside him. Soon, he vowed, he'd get to burrow himself into her softness and her heat, to merge body, soul, and extrasense. Very soon.

Morgan kissed Arthur with everything within her as he walked them back to his bedroom, her fear of rejection blasted away by the onslaught of need. She wanted this man with a voraciousness that left her as breathless as his kisses did. Everything, every touch, glance, conversation, and moment shared, had led up to this moment, to kissing him like this, holding him like this, wanting him like this.

With careful, gentle movements, he set her on her feet. That was as far as gentleness went. She reached for him, yanking his T-shirt over his head. It went flying, then he grasped her robe, slipping it from her with the quick flourish of a magician pulling a tablecloth. With another deft movement, her panties went flying to join the rest of her clothing in she-didn't-care-where.

He guided her back and down to the bed. Only then did he pause to stare at her, his eyes incandescent blue as they raked her from head to toe. "Beautiful," he grounded out. "So damned beautiful. Too beautiful to be believed."

His voice and his gaze stole her breath a moment before his mouth against hers actually did. Sparks danced behind her eyelids and along her skin, as he leisurely blazed a trail down her throat until his mouth joined his hand at her breast. She squirmed with pleasure as his tongue raked over her nipple with light strokes, circling, flicking, teasing, and torturing the distended tip. Her body tightened, her senses focused on that one pinpoint of sensation. Then he lightly bit down, giving her a sharp impression of teeth before sucking her nipple into his mouth.

Her body bucked against him as her thighs fell open, as if he'd found some magic key to unlock her sex. Magic hummed around them, between them, and in them, sliding against each other but not joined. Not yet.

He smiled against her breast. "Is that a demand for more?"

That wicked laugh tightened something deep inside her. "Yes," she hissed out. "More."

He immediately obliged, repeating the decadent deluge with her other breast. She gripped his shoulders, her body moving against his in a desperate quest for more. More touches, more kisses, more everything. Their magics swirled, thickening around them. More of that too.

Arthur kissed his way down her belly, his leisurely pace replaced by a more direct and focused march toward his prize. If he did that same move on her clit, she would—

His tongue flicked over her clit as his finger slipped inside her. She mewled like a kitten, her shields holding firm as if protecting her from the sensual onslaught. But Arthur was a force of nature not to be denied, a knight on a quest to deliver the promised pleasure, and he wouldn't stop until he succeeded.

Morgan's hands gripped his hair—to push him away or to draw him closer, she didn't know—as he inserted another finger inside her and began to move them in a slick, inexorable exploration. His tongue continued to lave her clitoris, wide sweeps interspersed with flicking attacks that wound her body tighter, and drove her higher.

Her hips moved involuntarily, helping him fuck her with his fingers. He thrust into her again, his fingers curving up to find her sweet spot. Then he sucked on her clit and her world fragmented, her body arching against his mouth, her thighs closing like a trap around his head. He moved his hands to cup her buttocks as she came, his tongue spearing inside her as he lapped her up, bringing her down by minute degrees.

Dimly she was aware of him rolling away, the sound of a condom being ripped open. She returned to herself enough to take the condom away from him before she pushed him onto his back. "You're not the only one who can be bossy," she told him, her voice sounding gritty to her ears as she wrapped her hand around him. "My turn to tease you."

"Tease me later," he demanded, lightning in his eyes. "I need inside you now."

She couldn't deny his demand since it was what she wanted too, wanted more than anything at that moment. She acceded to his request in her own way, taking her time rolling the condom down his shaft.

His eyes blazed as she straddled him, one hand on his thickness, the other balancing herself. "Lower your shields, Morgan," he demanded on a guttural whisper. "Let me feel all of you."

Lowering her shields, she then eased herself down onto him, caught by the desire firing his gaze as he watched her join them together. Magic flared around them in a visible flash of light. She gasped as her extrasense fully awakened, a blissful burst of magic, power, and emotion that set her entire body ablaze.

She began to ride him in earnest, grinding down on him, throwing her head back in eye-rolling pleasure. She was feeling as if she was outside herself, inside herself, beside herself with pure sensual bliss. Arthur shoved a hand between their bodies, his thumb caressing her clit. Stroke, circle, stroke, causing her to clamp down on him. He groaned, and she would swear that she could feel what he felt, feel her muscles gripping him in a decadent massage. His thumb stroked her again, but it was the brush of his extrasense against the sensitive bundle of flesh that had her seeing stars as she came again.

As if her orgasm was a signal, he flipped her onto her back, hooked her right leg, then plunged inside her. Mutual groans filled the room as their extrasense merged and locked. Need rode her hard, her hips thrusting up to meet his frenzied pace. Despite coming twice, she wanted more of him, needed more of him. Desperate moans clawed up her throat as she clawed at his back. He buried his face into the crook of her neck, his thrusts frenzied, wild.

Pressure built as their combined magic swelled, spiraling higher and higher until the pleasure couldn't be contained, constrained, or restrained. Her sex clamped down on him as waves of pleasure threw her head back, arching her off the bed as the third orgasm claimed her. He pistoned in and out again and again as if helpless to do anything else. Just when she didn't think she could take anymore, his body stiffened against hers, her name a curse, a prayer, and a plea against her throat.

After a moment, he got up to dispose of the condom. She instantly felt his absence, her inner muscles already missing the feel of him inside her. Then he returned to her, tucking her close against his side. Their combined extrasense flowed over and in her, and for a few precious moments, everything was perfect in her world. His heartbeat was a lullaby sending her into blissful slumber.

Chapter Thirteen

Morgan looked around Meg's backyard with nervous anticipation. The number of Light witches and healers that had shown up to support them awed and humbled her. Sure, she could see a large gathering of Light witches at every major Lafayette get-together, but this group had volunteered to help Morgan.

Five healers had answered Meg's call, and aside from her grandmother and her parents, six Lafayettes, each known for the strength of their extrasense, had come to help. While all Lafayettes had extrasense to varying degrees, not all would be considered Light witches. Only those who had been selected by her grandmother for this important event. They were all there to help, but Morgan knew that in the end, it all came down to her and her choices.

Though she supposed that everyone had agreed to come not only to help her but also to gawk at the Shadowchaser. As far as Morgan knew, few people had the chance to meet a Shadowchaser in an official capacity. They were the "when all else fails" option, as Morgan and her family knew from experience. Usually, a Shadowchaser's appearance meant that something big was about to go down, something that involved Shadow and was sure to involve a body count. While Morgan knew exactly what sort of Shadow calamity they were about to face, she hoped with all her being that the only body count would be the Shadowling lurking on the astral plane.

A low murmur of excitement and unease filled the air. Morgan turned to see Kira and Khefar walking from the direction of Mortimer Forest and the standing stones. Both were dressed in black trench coats which, Morgan supposed, probably made it easier to hide their weapons.

Morgan swallowed down a frisson of fear as the pair headed her way. This made her third time seeing the Shadowchaser after yesterday's introductions to her family and Meg, but that didn't make the meeting any less fraught. If anything, the energy that flowed from Kira and Khefar had her hindbrain screaming and her muscles tensing with the need to flee. Only Arthur's hand on her shoulder kept her anchored.

Arthur greeted Kira as affably as he had before, from one business acquaintance to another. Morgan managed a nod. The dark glasses that Kira wore despite the deepening dusk only made her seem more otherworldly. No one tried to shake hands, not even her overly demonstrative mother. The night wasn't about pleasantries, and they all knew it.

Kira turned to Meg and Tanya, both dressed in ceremonial robes appropriate for the Winter Solstice ritual. "I can sense the power of the standing stones, even from here," Kira said. "How many of the people gathered here are capable of accessing it?"

"We performed a short ritual at the stones earlier," Meg explained. "Everyone had a chance to introduce themselves to the stones and to ask the Light to bless them with the power needed today."

"We also had everyone tap into the ley lines running between here and the stones to test their connection," Tanya added. "They all managed to varying degrees. I believe the ritual will strengthen that connection, so we should have all the power you need. Is there anything specific that you need us to do?"

"Cast your circle as you normally do and conduct your Solstice ritual," Kira answered. "We'll use that power to help us on the astral plane. If we're not back before you finish the ritual, I'll need the matriarch and Meg to monitor us while Tanya holds the circle. Under no circumstances should the circle be broken before we return."

"Understood," Meg said with a sharp nod. "We'll go inform the others and prepare for the ritual."

"Arthur," her father called. "Let's review our game plan one more time."

"Yes, sir."

Morgan watched them walk off. Their meeting the day before had gone as well as she'd hoped as they'd bonded over traveling and their concern for her wellbeing. Neither wanted her to go to the astral plane, but everyone knew there wasn't another option that would guarantee catching the Shadowling's attention.

She turned to the Chaser, who was standing with Khefar and silently observing the final preparations. "Kira, may I ask you something?"

The Shadowchaser stepped closer. "What is it, Morgan?"

"I've been thinking." Morgan turned her back to the gathering, not wanting anyone to read her expression or her lips. "The Shadowblight, uhm, Shadowling. Would it be easier to kill it here than on the astral plane?"

Caution crept into Kira's eyes. "From what I saw in your memories, it must have lost the corporeal form that attacked you and retreated to the astral plane. It's energy there, so it will be more difficult to subdue it there, especially since yesterday was the first time I ever traveled to the astral plane. The physical plane is my hunting ground. The astral plane is not. I'll be at a disadvantage, but it's nothing I can't overcome."

"So that means that it would be better for you if it were here, right?" Morgan pressed. "If it had physical form?"

Both Kira and the taciturn warrior narrowed their gazes at her, and Morgan fought to ignore the goosebumps that rose along her arms. It was Khefar who spoke. "You wish to become a host to that Shadowling to bring it here, and you don't want either Arthur or your father to know this in advance."

"That's right."

Khefar turned to Kira. "This is now the best option. You're stronger here."

Morgan spoke before Kira could. "Does that mean we can do it?"

"Can we? Yes. Should we?" Kira sighed. "Your father and Arthur won't be happy about this, and it won't be you that they'll be angry with. They'll blame me."

"I'll make it so that it seems like a split-second decision on my part," Morgan said. "I was going to keep it to myself, then thought it would be better if you knew. Besides, I need you to tell me how to break the seal you put on me. Once we get through this, I'll take the blame, and you'll take the credit."

"Thank you for keeping me in the loop," Kira answered, her tone dry. She shook her head. "It takes a special talent to make something so dangerous sound like something so benign. Is that a quirk of your extrasense or a Lafayette thing?"

"Trust me, I know this isn't the same as taking a stroll along River Street. I'm terrified right now. I'm just trying not to think about how scared I am." She looked at the Shadowchaser, rubbing her hands together to warm them. "So, what do you think? Does this mean that you'll go along with my idea?"

"Is there a more effective one?" Kira asked. "Killing the Shadowling here will be much easier than trying to kill it on a non-physical plane, but you must be fully aware of what you're asking me to consent to. Do you truly understand what you're asking to do?"

Morgan nodded. "I'm asking you to allow the Shadowling to infect me completely, then drag me back to this plane so that you can get rid of it."

"All right. Do you realize how dangerous this is? You'll be fighting Shadow inside your own body, and it will be a lot worse than the blight you've been fighting all this time. Extracting it isn't going to be easy on you, either. This could go horribly wrong."

"I know." Morgan balled her hands into fists. Yeah, she was scared. How could she not be? Facing the creature that had harmed her and Penny. Inviting it inside her, hoping like hell she could keep it at bay long enough to return to the physical realm so that Kira could eliminate it. There were so many ways the plan could go sideways and only one way for it to go right.

She looked at her family, at Meg and Arthur. "I have faith, faith in myself, and faith in you. I have faith enough for all of us. I have so much to live for, and I need to be wholly myself. I'm not going to be defeated by Shadow."

Kira held Morgan's gaze far longer than the latter was comfortable with, but she persisted. If Morgan couldn't handle a staring contest with the Shadowchaser, how would she handle a confrontation with a Shadowling?

Finally, Kira snorted. "I'm impressed, Morgan Lafayette. You've either taken leave of your senses, or you're made of sterner stuff than I had initially thought."

"While the state of my senses could be hotly debated, I'm going to take it as a compliment." Morgan laughed. "Speaking of taking leave of my senses, can you remove the seal now? We should probably do that before we go, while there aren't too many eyes focused on us, right?"

"Khefar."

At once, the large man moved, placing his back to them and blocking them from most of the gathering. Kira stripped the glove from her right hand. "A quick touch should do it. Hold out your hand."

Morgan complied as Kira called her extrasense, a strong surge of power that Morgan was sure everyone in the village with any sensitivity could feel. Morgan had thought her grandmother powerful, but this, this was above Light Adept level.

The Chaser's hand glowed teal-white as she touched Morgan's fingertip with her own. A current of power ran up Morgan's arm to her shoulder, then stopped with a pop that she felt more than heard. A short wave of nausea upset her equilibrium, but she planted her feet and swallowed it down.

Kira pulled her glove back on. "We're done."

"Okay." Morgan drew in a fortifying breath. "There's one more thing I'd like to ask you."

"What now? You want to borrow my Lightblade?"

"What? No. Wait, can I do that?"

Kira stared her down. "You most certainly cannot do that."

"Okay then." Morgan smiled. "What I would like, when this is all over, is to get your phone number."

"My phone number?"

"Yeah. When I'm in Atlanta, or you swing through Savannah, we can meet up. We can bitch about our jobs. We can gush about our boyfriends. We can just hang out and talk over glasses of tea or wine. You know, like friends do."

Kira blinked. "You want to be friends. With me? A Shadowchaser that your family makes into a boogeyman?"

Ouch. "Well, to be fair, it was your predecessor, not you. And I'm not afraid of you now. I mean, I am, but not in a pee-my-pants sort of way. It's just...look, you didn't have to seal me. You didn't even have to agree to Arthur's request to hear about my problem. And now you're volunteering to go to the astral with us to take on a Shadowling."

Morgan shook her head. "Sure, that last part is part of your job, but sealing the Shadowblight and giving Arthur and me two stress-free days to focus on nothing but each other? I can never thank you enough for that. The least I can do is keep you in tea and coffee and conversation for as long as we both shall live."

A nervous laugh bubbled up along with the acid in her stomach. "Look at me, rambling on like a fool when we've got more important things to do right now. Sorry about that."

"Do you have your phone on you?"

"I do." Morgan pulled her phone out of her back pocket.

Kira also reached into her back pocket to extract her phone. "Here."

Morgan held her smartphone out, collecting Kira's contact information. "This is so cool!"

"It goes without saying that you shouldn't give my personal number to anyone, not even your father," Kira told her. "Not even your grandmother. They can reach me through Gilead."

"Gotcha." Morgan wondered how many people had Kira's personal contact information. She had a feeling it wasn't many, but the people who did were probably amazing. She'd hold the information close like the treasure it was.

"What are you ladies talking about?" her father asked as he joined them, Arthur following close behind.

"Just some secret girl stuff," Morgan answered, giving her dad a tight hug. "If I told you, not only would it not be a secret anymore, but it would also break girl code."

"Light forbid you break the secretive girl code." Her father returned the hug just as tightly, then dropped a kiss to her forehead. "We're going to get rid of this Shadowling and the blight inside you. We're going to do everything we can and then do some more."

"I know, Dad," she whispered, her throat tightening. "We're going to beat this thing and have even more reason to celebrate."

He stepped back from her, blinking rapidly. "It's almost time, so finish up your conversation. I'm going to go talk to your mother."

"I'm going to talk to Khefar for a moment," Kira told her. "See you at the circle."

Arthur turned to Morgan as Kira and Khefar walked away. He had no idea what the two women had talked about, but he'd felt Kira's flare of power and was certain it was more than girl code stuff. The need to ask welled inside him, but if Morgan didn't tell her father, she probably wouldn't tell him either. Still, he tried. "So, what were you really discussing with Kira?"

"Meeting up for drinks if she's ever in Savannah or if I'm ever in Atlanta," Morgan answered, then waved her phone. "And you're not the only one with a Shadowchaser's private number, so there."

"That makes you even more special." He spread his arms, needing to hold her. "Come here."

She pocketed her phone with a soft smile then stepped forward, slipping her arms around his waist and settling her cheek on his shoulder. Waves of emotion threatened to drag him under, and all he could do to hold on was to hold onto Morgan, hold on and hope like hell he'd be able to keep the promise he'd made to her father, to save Morgan no matter what happened to everyone else.

"There's so much I want to say to you. So much I want to do with you."

"The same goes for me, too," she whispered against his collarbone, her tone thick. "Thank you for these past few days. Even with everything going on, you've made me very happy. I'm so glad I met you."

He swallowed the lump in his throat, trying to overcome an encroaching sense of dread. "There's something I need to tell you before we step inside that circle."

She gazed up at him, eyes soft, coils caught in a light breeze. "What? Is it something bad? If so, you can tell me after, unless you need to tell me something embarrassing like my fly is open."

"No, it's not that." He reached up, brushing a lock of hair back from her eyes. He wanted to clearly see her reaction when he said the words. "It's not the right time to say this, but I can't think of a better time. I love you, Morgan."

Her smile was like dawn breaking after the longest night. "I think this is the perfect time to say it."

"I want you to promise me something. Promise me tomorrow. Can you do that? Can you promise me that much?"

She nodded, but he needed more than that. He needed her words. Taking a step back, he cupped her cheeks. "Promise me tomorrow."

A solemn gaze wreathed her features. "Tomorrow. I promise you tomorrow."

"All right then." He pressed a slow kiss to her forehead. "Let's go evict some Shadow from our astral plane."

Chapter Fourteen

The hairs on the back of Morgan's neck rose as the circle was cast. She called her extrasense, its response sluggish. A curtain of Light magic surrounded them, the bright greenish white ley lines running like electrical cords between them and the standing stones deep in the forest beyond Meg's yard. Her extrasense welcomed the mass of power but so did the blight, reawakening with an insistent hunger.

They didn't have much time. She especially didn't have much time. She could feel the blight pulling at her, straining toward the concentrated power of the circle, more powerful than it had been before Kira had sealed it. As soon as she reached the astral, she was certain the blight would call for the rest of itself, the Shadowling it belonged to. It would happen whether they wanted it to or not. She was also certain that it would want to return to the physical plane. She just had to make sure Kira was waiting for it when she returned.

She watched as her father closed his eyes. Khefar looked to Kira for a moment before following suit. Morgan called her extrasense, its response still listless now that the blight had been unsealed. Her senses crackled as she felt her father's astral form float up and out of his body. Then she felt something dark but not Shadow. Was that Khefar's astral form? Curiosity overwhelmed her. Why was his essence so dark? Not Shadow-filled, but not Light-absent either, just...different, different from any form she'd ever sensed before.

Then Arthur closed his eyes, and she felt him rise out of his physical form. This time she focused on Kira, her astra senses picking up the blue-white of the Shadowchaser's astral form. It flickered not unlike the standing stones, purple-white with flashes of green. Did that mean that Kira was also tainted by Shadow? It was bound to happen, Morgan supposed, considering Kira's job. Then again, could a Shadowchaser remain a Chaser if they had Shadow inside them?

Morgan shook her head. That wasn't what she needed to focus on, no matter how badly she wanted to distract herself. She needed to focus. Her literal life depended on what happened next.

Taking deep, even breaths, Morgan calmed her nerves and centered herself. Sliding her eyes closed, she focused on the silvery cord that rooted her astral form to the physical world. She visualized herself floating free of her body, surprised with how easy it was compared to just a few days before. She pushed free of her body, then looked down at herself sitting in a lawn chair next to Arthur. Kira sat next to him beside Khefar, with Morgan's father sitting in the last chair. Their astral bodies hovered in the state between the physical and dreaming planes, aura-focused outlines of themselves.

Relief flooded Morgan as they all made it safely to the dream plane. Her father and Arthur had practiced taking the warrior and the Shadowchaser this far several times the day before but hadn't attempted the astral for fear of alerting the Shadowling. If traveling to the dream plane was this easily done, surely there wouldn't be a problem leveling up to the astral. "How should we do this?"

"I'll create a doorway between this plane and the astral one," her father answered. "I'll take Khefar first. Arthur will follow next with Kira, then you will bring up the rear. Or feel free to wait for us here. Better yet, wait in the circle."

"Dad, you know I can't do that. And I won't."

Darien Lafayette sighed. "What kind of father would I be if I didn't want to keep my child safe?"

"What kind of woman would I be if I just let others save me while I sit on my ass and do nothing?" she countered. "You didn't raise me to be that way."

"Ouch." Her father clutched his heart, then smiled sadly. "It was worth a try."

He cleared his throat, then channeled more of his extrasense to his hands to sketch the outline of an entryway to the next plane. Dreamers floated around them, most of them human, although there were some dogs chasing squirrels. None of the dreamers paid attention to their group, thank the Light. The last thing they needed was lucid dreamers being overly curious about their activities.

"Be careful, Dad."

"Always." Her father linked hands with Khefar then took a step toward the portal. They were immediately blocked by an invisible barrier. He tried again, only to receive the same result. When he released his hold on the warrior, her father was able to step through.

Her father turned to them with a frown. "Arthur, you try with Kira."

Here on the dreaming plane, they were more their physical selves than on the astral. Here, Kira—and her extrasense—were nearly the same, just less corporeal, meaning the gloves she used didn't exist on the dreaming plane. So how had Arthur brought her back to the physical plane?

Kira raised her left hand. The energy around it appeared to drain down her arm, leaving the hand bare. At her nod, Arthur clasped her hand and guided them to the doorway. Just as with Morgan's father and Khefar, only Arthur could breach the passage.

"Dammit," Darien Lafayette swore. "I was afraid this might happen."

"What?" Morgan asked. "Why can't they go to the astral plane?"

"Probably because your father is used to guiding normal humans, and Khefar and I aren't your average humans," Kira explained with a sharp smile. "We thought it might be difficult to travel that far, but not impossible."

"We didn't have enough time to properly prepare either of you for the journey," her father said, frustration settling into his features. "People train for months, even years, to learn how to travel. It could be dangerous for us if we try to force our way through."

"We don't have that kind of time," Arthur pointed out. "What's our Plan B?"

Morgan looked to Kira, who gave her a small nod. "There's only one way left," she said, her voice hushed by fear. "I have to go get it."

Her father stepped forward. "Morgan, don't even think—"

"Twenty-five percent of that thing is already in me, Dad," Morgan interrupted. "If I don't do this, I'll die. If I do this, I could die, but if I don't, that thing will take me over at some point, and there might not be a Shadowchaser with Kira's mindset around to save me. Better to do this right now, on our terms, instead of going back empty-handed with a death sentence over my head."

Without another word, she stepped through the doorway. A trumpeting cry filled the air, a ripple of malevolent energy that buffeted her like waves roused by a storm. Terror threatened to drown her. She swallowed it down and dropped her shields, turning herself into a beacon.

"Come on, you piece of shit, Shadowling!" she shouted into the void. "You want the rest of your essence? You want to get back to the physical world? Then come at me, you son of a bitch!"

She didn't have to wait long. Yellow light coalesced on the horizon, resolving itself into a giant astral serpent. It sped toward her, mouth wide and bearing fangs.

"Light protect me," Morgan prayed, fear dousing her anew. It had hurt like hell when the Shadowling had attacked her the first time, before she'd undergone the painful sealing ritual with Kira. She braced herself for the pain she knew would come.

"Morgan, no!" Arthur stepped in front of her, a gleaming white knight, his mental and astral shields blocking her from the approaching creature.

"I have to do this, Arthur. You know I do." Morgan gave him a smile. "I love you. I'm counting on you to be my anchor and my knight one more time. Kira's waiting to deal with the Shadowling. Make sure I get back. After all, I did promise you tomorrow, right?"

Before he could reply, she rushed around him and spread her arms wide as the embodiment of everything she stood against barreled into her. She screamed at the burst of pain just before she was swept away by yellow-tinged blackness.

Chapter Fifteen

"**M**organ!"

Horror filled Arthur as he helplessly watched the Shadow serpent burrow its way into Morgan's astral body. She screamed again, her astral form convulsing as it fought against the incursion. He rushed to her, catching her just as she collapsed.

"Take me back," she ground out in a voice unlike her own. "Hurry!"

He held Morgan's astral body in his arms, visualizing their soul cords, reeling them down through the different planes of existence back to their physical world. He opened his eyes to find Kira, Khefar, and Darien Lafayette surrounding Morgan's chair. Heart in his throat, he leaped out of his chair and raced to Morgan's side.

"It's in her, the damned thing's in her." Terror unhinged his knees as he dropped to the ground beside her. "Can you get it out?"

Kira snatched off her gloves. "I'm going to try."

"Try?" Darien Lafayette echoed. "You better do more than try."

"The 'try' part is keeping Morgan alive while I destroy the Shadowling trying to make her its host," Kira snapped back. "You do want your daughter to live, right?"

"Save her. Please save her." Darien blew out a broken breath. "What do you need us to do?"

"Right now, we need to physically and magically restrain her. The Shadowling wants to run. We can't let it leave this circle. Let's lay her on the ground for now."

Arthur hurriedly pulled off his coat and spread it on the ground before helping her father lay Morgan down. "Arthur, get on her right side, hold her down," Kira ordered. "Khefar, hold her left arm down, palm up. Lafayette, make sure the circle isn't broken. We need all the Light help we can get."

"Honey, what's wrong with Morgan?" Tanya Lafayette called. "What's wrong with my baby?"

"The Shadowchaser's helping her, sweetheart." Darien crossed to his wife. "She's going to remove the blight now. We need you, Meg, and the others to hold the circle so that it can't escape."

"Kira," Arthur called. "Look at Morgan."

Morgan lay panting, eyes open and fixed on the sky. As he watched, the white of her eyes bled to black, and the swirls of black vines he'd seen on her back now crawled across her face. Shadow magic seeped from her in smoke-like tendrils.

"Morgan." His voice broke. "Is she—is she—"

"I can feel her fighting Shadow," Kira cut in. "If you focus your extrasense, you can, too. I need you to dial down your fear and concentrate on Morgan. Can you do that for me? Can you do that for her?"

Arthur swallowed and fought to control his emotions. Nothing, not even his fear, mattered. Only saving Morgan did. He'd do whatever

Kira needed him to do as long as Morgan survived. "Yes. Whatever you need, I'll do it."

"Ar...thur..."

He could barely hear Morgan's voice over the thudding of his heart. He clasped her hand tightly, leaning over to better hear her. "I'm here, love. I'm right here."

A grimace constricted her features as she groaned. "D-don't let it...kick me out."

"I won't, I swear. You promised me tomorrow, right? I'm not going to let anything or anyone take you away from me."

Belle Lafayette approached them. "I can provide my power."

Kira shook her head. "Hopefully, it won't come to that. Arthur is closely connected to Morgan. Plus, he can draw power from the circle and the standing stones if need be. Are you listening, Arthur?"

When he nodded, Kira continued, "When I start, I need all of you, especially the astral travelers, to keep your shields locked down. The Shadowling may try to jump into another host."

The Shadowchaser slid her Lightblade free of its sheath with a silver sibilant sound. She whispered a few words in a language he didn't understand. Power rose on a magic wind, power as strong as the combined circle, more power than he'd ever witnessed in one person before. Even without his extrasense, he could see the glow of Kira's power, outlining her body with an ultraviolet light. Murmurs rose to shocked gasps as the Shadowchaser's Lightblade brightened to starlight, to moonlight, to concentrated sunlight.

"Khefar."

"I am here."

Kira glanced at the other man, and even in the darkness, Arthur could see something profound and unspoken pass between them. With a nod, Kira returned her attention to Morgan. Before Arthur could guess her intention, the Shadowchaser raised her blade high and swung down, embedding the dagger into Morgan's palm through her lifeline.

Morgan shrieked, an inhuman sound that silenced everyone. Her body bowed as if struck by an electrical current, then began to struggle, attempting to break free of their hold.

"Immobilize her!"

Arthur followed Kira's command, moving to put his full weight on Morgan's legs while still holding her hand. Khefar held her left arm down. She growled in response, snapping at them both. She was a lot stronger with a Shadowling fighting to control her body. Arthur's heart clanged at the knowledge that Morgan was in pain, that she was suffering. He almost begged Kira to stop but choked the need down and pulled his resolve together. Stopping now would certainly mean death for Morgan and probably inflict some damage on the Shadowchaser, too. Neither would happen, not while he had Light to give.

"Arthur." Kira's tone sounded like rocks grinding together. "Now the hard part really begins. We're going to fight the Shadowling on two fronts. My Lightblade and I will fight the Shadowling head-on. I'm drawing it to me to destroy it. It will take as long as it needs to. What I need you to do is use your extrasense to keep your connection with Morgan open and channel as much Light as you can. I need you to push as much Light as you can into her body, like giving her a blood transfusion. This is going to be hard on you and harder on her, but I need you to stand firm. You're the only one who can do this. If you can't handle it, buck up and do it anyway. Understood?"

"Understood." Arthur closed his eyes and locked his shields in place, focusing his extrasense on Morgan. He reached out with his entire being, physically, magically, and psychically, until he felt the weak pulse of her extrasense. "Morgan."

"I...feel you." Her response was an echo of a whisper. "It's trying to devour my Light."

"I won't let it. We won't let it."

He latched onto her extrasense, then pushed some of his Light at her. The Shadowling struck at him, beating at Arthur's shields. "This body is mine. MINE!"

"This body is not yours," Arthur growled. "It is Morgan's and Morgan's alone."

He pushed more Light into Morgan through their connection. "That's right, you bastard. I'm not going to let you take her away from me."

He tightened his grip on Morgan's right hand, leaning over to rest his forehead on their entwined fingers. The damp chill soaked into him; he ignored it, tears blurring his vision as he pushed more of his extrasense to her. "Morgan, stay with us. I know you want to. I'm right here. I'll help you fight."

Her hand flexed in his. He gasped in relief. She was still there, still fighting.

Kira muttered something. He wasn't sure if it was a prayer or something else. Khefar shifted closer to her, his gaze on Kira. The Chaser's Lightblade pulsed like a heartbeat as it siphoned off the Shadow creature. No, more like it devoured the thing, swallowing Shadow magic in distressingly slow increments. Tendrils of what looked like yellow-black smoke pooled where the blade pierced Morgan's palm.

Sweat beaded Kira's forehead, and her expression pinched with what looked like painful concentration. The ultraviolet glow around her now took on a hint of a greenish tinge. Was the Lightblade using her body to dissipate the Shadowling?

Arthur frowned, worry pulling at him. The Shadowchaser had called up an enormous amount of power to save Morgan. Did she have enough strength to make it through? Was the Chaser running out of the energy needed to separate the Shadowling from Morgan before destroying it?

"Do you need some of my energy, Kira? I can pull more Light."

"Kira can tap into the standing stones if need be," Khefar told him. "I'll help her. Keep your focus on Morgan."

Arthur took the other man's words as the warning they were, belatedly remembering that he'd never so much as shook Kira's bare hand in all the time that he'd known her. Given that she was essentially using her ability to siphon the blight from Morgan, he was better off not trying to share energy with the Shadowchaser.

"Keep feeding Light energy into Morgan," Kira urged, her voice as strained as her expression. "The more Light you give her, the less this Shadowling will be able to hide, and its hold on Morgan will weaken even more. We'll burn this bastard at both ends until it lets Morgan go."

"Right." He returned his attention to Morgan. She wasn't physically struggling as much as she had before, so he stretched out beside her, unmindful of the cold ground, and clasped his hand between both of his. Resting his forehead against their hands, he could still feel their connection, still feel her fighting to hold onto herself while keeping the Shadowling from engulfing her. He linked with her completely, shielding a distant memory as he reached out past the circle to tap into the ley lines running from the stone circle in Mortimer Forest. Please help us. Please help us help Morgan.

A warm wind blew through his body as the ley lines and the stones responded. He could sense the lines glowing brighter, sending Light coursing through him in gleaming waves. He drew in as much as he could, as much as his body could hold, then drew in more. He, in turn, sent it to Morgan, visualizing it flooding her system. Light flowed down her arm into her torso, some coursing down to her legs, some going to her head as if soaking into her veins and arteries. She whimpered—no, the Shadowling did, its hold on her weakening.

"The markings on her face are receding," Khefar announced. "Whatever you're doing, keep it up."

Heat swamped Arthur as he continued to pour Light into Morgan, seeing it pool in her chest, surrounding her heart, bathing it in a golden-white glow. Her fingers flexed against his again as he felt her extrasense reaching for him, reaching for the Light. "That's it," he urged her. "The Light embraces you. The Light protects you. The Light gives you strength to stand against all things Shadow."

As if a dam had broken, more power deluged him, engulfing his body until it burned. He surrendered willingly, gritting his teeth against the pressure of power that battered his body and his extrasense. It barreled through him and into Morgan, blowing their connection wide open. Even with his eyes closed, he knew their bodies glowed with Light, brightening the areas around them to midday. So much Light that even the Shadowling couldn't devour, couldn't hide, couldn't survive.

It could have been hours or minutes; Arthur couldn't tell. The only thing he knew for certain was that his connection with Morgan was strong, stronger than it had been when they'd first started the ordeal. Maybe even stronger than when they'd first met. He couldn't sense any trace of Shadow between them, only pure Light surrounding them, supporting them, and surging through them.

Dimly he heard someone calling his name, urging him to release his hold. He opened his eyes, but all he could see was golden-white light. "Morgan. Is Morgan safe?"

"She's safe." Belle Lafayette's voice sounded like a whisper in a storm. "You can let go now, son."

He did, and finally, darkness claimed him.

Chapter Sixteen

"Mom! I can't breathe! At least let me go to the bathroom before you try to squeeze the life out of me like this!"

"No!" Morgan's mother hugged her harder, rocking back and forth. "My baby girl is alive. You were fighting Shadow so hard, and I couldn't do anything to help. You scared me to death!"

Morgan stopped resisting and rubbed her mother's back to reassure her. "It's okay, Mom. I'm sorry."

"You should be sorry," her father retorted, his voice thick. "You willingly allowed yourself to be possessed by a Shadowling. You barely survived. If the Shadowchaser hadn't been there..."

Her father didn't have to finish the thought. They all knew that, without Kira's help, the Shadowling would have consumed her.

Morgan extracted herself from her mother's embrace as gently as she could. "But Kira was there, and I'm alive. I'm alright."

Worry still etched her mother's features. "How do you feel?"

"Lighter. I didn't realize how weighed down I felt with the blight in me. Now I feel better than I did even before I was attacked."

With her parents' expressions still too full of concern, Morgan changed the subject. "What day is it? Where are Kira and the others? I'm assuming we're still at Meg's house, but I don't remember much of anything after coming back from the astral plane."

"That's because you had a Shadowchaser and a Shadowling playing tug-of-war with your body," her mother replied, then sighed. "Kira and Mr. Tall, Dark, and Scary left while we were trying to heal you and Arthur."

"Arthur?" Panic swelled as she threw back the bedcovers. "Why did he need healing? What happened to him? Where is he?"

Both parents held out their hands to stop her from getting out of bed. Then her father spoke. "He's in the room next door, recovering like you. Arthur pulled so much Light energy from the ley lines trying to save you that he nearly burned himself out, and you went from almost being lost to Shadow to almost being lost to Light."

Morgan recalled the overwhelming chill of darkness trying to rip her soul apart chunk by chunk, a sibilant voice urging her to give up. Desperately reaching for her tenuous connection to Arthur. Then, she was inundated with Light, obliterating shadow and cleansing her soul. There was more Light than she'd ever accessed before.

Surely, Arthur had saved her as much as Kira had. Just thinking of him brought their connection into focus, and she could sense that he was safe. That and the fact that he was sleeping kept her from pushing past her parents to find him. "He's okay, just sleeping. It must have taken a lot of Light for him and Kira to save me."

Her mother nodded. "After the Shadowling was destroyed, the two of you glowed like candles for nearly three hours. Ma Belle was the only Adept with enough power to even touch either of you, but healing isn't her strength. All she could do was get Arthur to release his hold on the ley lines and physically separate you two."

"Even then, we weren't sure if separating you was enough to stop the feedback loop of power," her father added. "It was as if your extrasense had merged. The healers couldn't assess either of you until you stopped glowing from the remnants of that power surge."

"It's been two days," her mother said, a warble in her voice. "Both of you have been asleep for two days."

"Two days?" Morgan forced herself to math. That meant it was the day before Christmas Eve. She and Arthur had missed the ball at the castle. Although she was disappointed that she wouldn't get to wear the ball gown, she was happier that she was alive to be disappointed. "Where's Ma Belle? She wasn't hurt, was she?"

"She's fine," her father answered. "Once we knew you and Arthur were out of danger, she and the cousins flew back to Savannah to get ready for the Christmas festivities."

"I'm glad." Morgan sank back against the pillows, then sat up again. "Wait. Why are you in a suit? Are you doing Gilead work here?"

It was her mother who answered. "Your father has had to spend time debriefing Gilead agents on both sides of the Atlantic about what happened during the solstice. I don't know if Shadowchasers have jurisdictions, but apparently, our efforts to save you caused a lot of bureaucratic red tape."

"Hmph." Morgan didn't try to find it within herself to care. Their previous lack of involvement with her case still rankled. "Now they want to be involved? I'm sorry they're making you work, Dad."

"Don't be. If I weren't here, other Gilead agents would be."

"Why?"

Her father frowned. "Any incident involving a Shadowchaser is a big deal and garners a tremendous amount of attention. Then there's the amount of Light that you and Arthur generated. We know some impact of that, but not all of the ramifications. Too many people are interested in you, in both of you, and I'm doing my level best to blunt that curiosity."

Morgan hugged herself. "Gilead being interested in us doesn't sound like fun, Dad."

"I know. Believe me, I know. Which is why I'd feel better if we returned to Savannah as soon as we can arrange a flight, hopefully sometime tomorrow. You'll be able to celebrate Christmas in Savannah like you wanted."

Dismay swept through Morgan. As much as she wanted to be home for the holidays, she wasn't ready to say goodbye to Arthur. She wasn't sure if she could say goodbye.

She swung her legs over the side of the bed. "I need to see Arthur. I can sense that he's okay, but I still want to see for myself."

"Wait." Her mother took her hand. "You said that you could sense that Arthur's fine. Could you sense him like this before?"

Morgan pursed her lips, thinking. "No," she said slowly. "Before we needed to touch for our extrasense to merge but sensing him like this is different."

Her parents exchanged glances, causing anxiety to sprout. Her father took a step closer. "Call your extrasense."

Morgan closed her eyes, then reached for her power. Her extrasense immediately flared, warmth flooding her system like premium liquor, different than before.

"I feel...not strange, but definitely different." She glanced at her father. "I didn't have to try to call my extrasense. It's like it was just there, ready and waiting for me. I..."

She broke off, staring at her hands. A golden glow surrounded them. "Dad?"

Her father touched her shoulder. "Your grandmother and Meg both thought something like this might happen."

"Something like what? Becoming a glow stick?"

"Power surges in your extrasense. We all think you and Arthur are more powerful now than you were before the solstice. It might take a while for your abilities to settle down into your new normal. Ma Belle, being the strongest Adept we know, will be able to help you find your balance. Right now, your power is unpredictable, which is another reason to go home sooner rather than later."

Reluctance tugged at Morgan, but she knew her father was right. If she couldn't control her extrasense it would be better to be back home surrounded by Lafayettes. But parting from Arthur so soon...

A knock sounded on the door a moment before it opened to reveal Arthur. Heedless of her parents, Morgan hurled herself out of bed and into Arthur's arms. Their extrasense flared instantly, wrapping around them like a warm and welcomed robe of light. Overcome, she pressed her face against his chest, reassured by the steady thump-thump of his heart. It was one thing to know he was safe from harm; it was another thing to see and hold him herself.

Her father coughed. "We'll give you kids some privacy, but we're going to need to talk soon."

Morgan nodded as her parents left, then pounded her fist against Arthur's chest. "You almost burned yourself out being a conduit of Light. What possessed you to do that?"

"I could ask you the same question, but I already know the answer." He buried his face into the crook of her neck as a shudder passed through him. "What would I have done if you didn't make it? I couldn't watch and not do something. So when Kira said to give you Light, I gave you Light. I would give anything to save you. Anything."

"You think I'd want you to sacrifice yourself?" She thumped his chest again. "You really think I'd be happy for you to exchange your life for mine?"

He hugged her tight enough to hurt, but she didn't mind. "We both sacrificed. We both came through. We're both here now."

"Arthur," she choked on his name as she admitted to him what she couldn't admit to her parents. "I was so scared."

"But you were also brave," he whispered in her ear, his voice tight. "I watched you fighting and struggling to hold out against that thing. You did what you had to do, and I did what I had to do to help so that Kira could safely pull that Shadowling out of you."

"Like channeling all that Light energy. Once again, my knight in shining armor, literally my light in the darkness." She stepped back to look at him, then blinked. "You are way more blond than I remember you being."

"As to that..." He pushed a hand through his now shockingly white-blond locks with a self-deprecating laugh. "Apparently, drawing in that much Light has consequences. You've got a new look as well."

"What?" She turned slowly, looking for a mirror in the unfamiliar room. She didn't have to step closer to her reflection to see a sprig of golden coils springing from the russet curls at her right temple. "I'm not sure if this look is Bride of Frankenstein or Cruella. Do I look old?"

"No." He stepped up behind her. "You look beautiful as always."

"I've been asleep for two days. My makeup's gone and look at my hair. I think holding all that energy burned your eyesight, too." She waved her hands. "Not that I'm looking for compliments, but..."

Once again, a glow enveloped her hands. She turned to face him, tucking her hands behind her. "Uhm, that's a new thing that's happening on its own."

He reached for her hands. That happy spark of recognition ignited between them as it had the first time they'd touched. It seemed forever ago that she'd stumbled into his antiquities shop, forever that they'd known each other.

"Our magics are kindred spirits," she murmured, running her thumbs across his knuckles.

"We pulled in a lot of power, not only from the circle our mothers cast but also the ley lines running to the standing stones. Some of that power remained with us. I think it's fair to say that we're much stronger than we were before."

"The question is, how strong, and will we be able to control it?" Sudden tears welled in her eyes. "I feel like I should apologize to you."

Alarm flashed through his gaze. "Apologize? For what?"

She sniffed, shrugging her shoulders helplessly. "I don't know. For barreling into your shop. For disrupting your life. For nearly getting you killed."

"Don't think like that, love." He used his knuckles to carefully wipe away the scattering of tears on her cheeks. "My life was in need of a good disruption, especially one as lovely as you. I'm forever grateful that I was able to meet you, though it was a close thing because I wasn't supposed to return to Caynham until after I met Kira in London. She was delayed, so we arranged to meet here. I believe I was meant to be here when you arrived."

"Even though all I've done is be a drain on you and your mother?" she choked out.

"Neither of us believe that, so don't you believe it either." He gently cupped her shoulders. "That's behind us now. The blight is gone. You have your future back."

She glanced down at her hands. The visible glow of her extrasense now reached her forearms. "A future of being my own personal flashlight? Not exactly what I'd planned."

His hands slid down her arms to entangle her fingers. "I don't think it will be like this forever."

She stepped back before she drew in a shaky breath. "Because of everything that's happened, my parents want to fly back home tomorrow. They want me to go back with them."

"Of course you should."

"Of course?" she echoed with a frown. "Why don't you sound the tiniest bit upset about us having to part, O man who professed his love?"

A smile lit his eyes. "Who said anything about us having to part?"

"But I'm leaving tomorrow."

"So you've said." He tightened his grip on her hands, his now glowing like hers. "Shouldn't the man who professed his love be wherever his love is?"

Hope sparked in her chest. "Are you coming with?"

"I'm coming with. My mother told me what's been going on with Gilead and our power. Your grandmother said that our extrasense rose several levels with all the Light we channeled. We may not be at Adept level, but she thinks we're awfully close. She said she could help us manage our extrasense. Frankly speaking, I'd much rather have Ma Belle test me than any of the bureaucrats from Gilead."

"How...how long do you think you'll stay in Savannah?"

"For as long as it takes," he answered. "If that's a month, a year, our lifetime...I'm aiming for lifetime, truth be told."

She gripped his biceps, hearing his words but not daring to believe them. Not yet. "But what about your shop?"

"Funny thing, that." Pure sunshine lit his features. "It actually runs better when I'm not there. My primary work isn't being in the shop. It's searching for bits and baubles for the shop and my clients, which takes me all over the globe. My base of operations could be anywhere, including Savannah."

"Really?"

"Really." His hands dropped to her waist, pulling her snug against him. "You're not thinking of breaking your promise, are you?"

"What promise?"

"Have you forgotten so soon? You promised me tomorrow, and my intention is to accept your offer."

The room brightened as joy welled up inside her. "You're right, I did promise. I feel like it should be pointed out that tomorrow has its own tomorrow. There's never not going to be a tomorrow."

"Your logic is impeccable." He kissed her nose before staring down at her with a solemn gaze. "Morgan Lafayette, will you do me the honor of giving me your tomorrows?"

"For as long as there are tomorrows, I'll give them to you."

"And I'll give you all of mine," he promised. "The best Christmas present I could ever hope for."

About the Author

S eressia Glass is an award-winning author of paranormal and contemporary romance as well as urban fantasy. She enjoys writing about themes of love and acceptance and believes everyone has a story to be told. She lives south of Atlanta with her guitar-wielding husband, their son, and two fur babies.

Would you like a FREE novella? Visit www.seressia.com and sign up for her newsletter. You can also visit her website to discover the first trilogy of Shadowchasers novels.